# Beauty and the Bossman

## Stephanie Renee

*This one goes out to my amazing husband--who always makes me feel like the prettiest girl in the world. Thank you, D, for loving me and all my jiggly parts. XOXO*

# Chapter One

## ROMY

"**M**ontgomery Construction. How may I help you?" I answer the phone with my usual false sincerity.

Grabbing my pen, I jot down some notes on my calendar about when the next shipment of lumber is due to arrive.

"Mmm-hmm. Okay, we will see you then," I say before hanging up the phone. I make a few additional notes and then vigorously rub my hands together in an attempt to keep them warm.

It's Minnesota in the middle of winter, though, so I don't think I'll officially thaw until Spring has sprung.

Every year, I tell myself I need to leave this frozen tundra and move somewhere warm, but here I sit—in this construction trailer, which doesn't do much to keep out the frigid air.

Why am I sitting in a construction trailer? Well, I'm the assistant to Aiden Montgomery, who owns Montgomery Construction. And instead of having a centralized office in a lovely warm office building, Mr. Montgomery insists on having a temporary office on whatever job site he's working on at any given time.

I don't know why he cares so much. He's not usually the one who spends all of his time in here. In fact, he's barely in here at all, always proclaiming he hates any type of paperwork.

That's where I come in.

I'm basically Mr. Montgomery's right hand—or left hand, depending on who you are, I guess. I handle most of the boring shit while he oversees all of the construction.

It might not be the most glamorous of jobs, but it pays pretty well, and as far as bosses go, Mr. Montgomery isn't a bad one.

Despite his slightly gruff nature, he's still a pretty nice guy. He also has these gorgeous eyes that would be pretty easy to get lost in. I mean, if I spent any time gazing into them—which I don't.

Grabbing my coat off the back of my chair, I pull it on and zip it up. Then, I tug my mittens out of my pocket and put those on too.

Even though I'm not skin and bones, I still get cold easily. My love handles and junk in the trunk do nothing to insulate me for warmth.

My mitten-covered hands reach up to cover my cold nose. I take a deep breath, finally starting to feel a little warmer. But as if right on cue, the door to the trailer swings open, letting a gust of wintery air sweep in.

Mr. Montgomery steps in before pulling the door shut behind him.

Hands still on my nose, I glare at him. He lumbers in, standing over six feet tall. He's a large man, but he always seems to be wearing multiple layers of clothing, so it's hard to tell exactly how large.

His eyes peer at me from under the baseball cap he always wears.

"You okay?" His low voice is somehow rough and silky smooth all at the same time.

"Cold," is all I say in response.

"We need to get you a little space heater," he says, walking over to his desk.

"You always say that," I mutter.

Holding a white paper bag, he walks toward me. When he

sets it on the desk in front of me, he says, "How about a peace offering?"

The moment I open the bag, the delicious smell of a toasted meatball sub fills my nostrils. And not just any meatball sub—my *favorite* meatball sub.

What can I say? After two and a half years of working together, the man knows what I like to eat for lunch—and what I want in my coffee. He's got that one memorized too.

He grabs his own sandwich out of the bag and walks over to his desk. "You might need to take off your mittens," he says in a typical smart-ass fashion.

I attempt to unwrap the sandwich with them still on to prove him and his snarky attitude wrong. But a few seconds in, I give up the fight and tug off the wool mittens. My growling stomach outweighs my cold hands.

The first bite makes me let out a small moan. When Mr. Montgomery shifts uncomfortably in his seat, my cheeks redden. Pushing my glasses up the brim of my nose, I avoid eye contact. Sometimes I'm too awkward for my own good. Call it a character flaw—one of many.

We eat our sandwiches in silence. Every once in a while, I can feel his eyes on me. His gaze is so intense that I don't need to look at him to feel it boring into me.

When he's done with his sandwich, he gets up to throw away his trash before walking over to me.

"I might have a solution to your cold problem," he begins.

I brace myself for him to mention a space heater again, but he doesn't.

Instead, he continues with, "In a couple of weeks, there's a construction conference going on. Well, it's sort of half conference, half retreat. There will be classes but still other fun stuff to do too. I wasn't planning on going, but they've asked me to speak at one of the seminars."

I fight the urge to ask him why in the hell they'd want *him* to be a guest speaker. The man barely speaks more than fifty words a day. But I don't interrupt him to say any of that.

He goes on, "Anyway, it's a week-long thing, and I'd like for you to come with me. It's a nice resort, and I'll cover the cost of your flights and the room stay. All the meals are included, and it's an open bar all week. And of course, you'd be able to take some classes while you're there if anything interests you."

I think about it for a moment. I've never been to any type of conference before, and I'm super intrigued to know what Mr. Quiet might say to a vast room full of people. But who's going to run this place?

When I ask him that very question, he answers with, "Tom can handle things while we're gone. The job on this site is winding down anyway, so I shouldn't be needed."

Tom is his number two when he's doing the construction side of things. He's a nice guy, but I guess I don't have the faith in him that our boss does.

My mind races a mile a minute, worrying about how much work will be piled up for me when I get back. But I suppose I could take my laptop and at least answer emails while I'm there.

Feeling his eyes still staring at me, I sigh and say, "Okay. Sounds great."

I swear I see a hint of a smile, but it disappears too quickly to know for sure.

"Perfect," he replies. "I'll send you all the details."

I nod, and he heads toward the door to get back to work, but I stop him.

"Wait, how does this whole thing help solve the problem of me being cold?"

Now, he actually smiles. A full, wholehearted smile. And before he walks out the door, he says, "Oh, did I not mention it's in Key West?"

# Chapter Two

## AIDEN

T he machines are so loud around me that I'm surprised I hear my phone ringing from my pocket.

When I pull it out, I see it's Allison calling. Allison is my twin sister, so we've always been close. That whole 'twin intuition' thing that people always talk about? It's a real thing.

"Hey, sis," I answer. "Hold on a minute."

I jog over to my truck and slide in. Thankfully, most of the noise outside is drowned out.

I put the phone back up to my ear. "Sorry about that; I couldn't hear. What's up?"

"Just checking in on my favorite little brother," she jokes.

"First of all, I'm your *only* brother. Second, you're only two minutes older than I am, and I'm like a foot taller than you. You can hardly call me your *little* brother."

"Yet, I still do," she laughs. "I'm going to be in town next weekend and wanted to see if you had time to do lunch with your wonderful sister."

Allison moved to New York to run her real-estate firm, so she's not back here in Minnesota too much. I feel awful that for once, I won't be in town to hang out with her, but when I explain about the conference, she's nothing but supportive.

"That's awesome, Aiden!" She exclaims. "When do you leave?"

"Romy and I fly out that Friday."

I can almost hear the smile in her voice as she asks, "Romy? Your assistant Romy?"

"Yeah. What about it?"

"Just wondering what's going to happen when you and your cute assistant are away from work and in a tropical paradise for a whole week."

I'm stuck on the fact that she called Romy cute. Immediately, my assistant's face pops into my head.

*Is she cute?*

Sure. But have I ever thought of her in that way? No. I've forced myself not to.

*Why?*

She's my assistant, and I believe in boundaries. Truth be told, I think of her as more than my assistant. Without her, this business wouldn't be what it is today. We've cultivated an excellent working relationship, and I don't want to ruin that just because my dick wants to play.

Besides, I'm pretty sure she feels the same way. She probably just thinks of me as her grumpy boss. I act like that, so we never get too close. And she shows up to work every day in her big glasses and messy bun. I don't think I've seen her hair down since I first interviewed her for the job.

"You still there?" Allison asks, pulling me from my thoughts.

*Damn, I forgot she was still on the phone.*

"Yeah, sorry. I got distracted watching one of my guys working."

"Uh-huh. Sure. You sure you weren't thinking about Romy?"

I sigh. "You're crazy if you think anything is going on there."

"I'm just saying that the beach does crazy things to people."

"Not me."

"Would it really be that bad for you to find a nice girl to

settle down with?" She asks.

"I could ask you the same thing."

"Aiden, I'm a lesbian living in New York City. I settle down with a new nice girl every weekend."

My laugh fills the cab of my truck. "Yeah, yeah. Just rub it in that you're getting more action than me."

"It's your own fault. All work and no play makes Aiden a horny boy."

I cringe. "Don't say the word 'horny.' It's weird."

"Prude," she mocks.

She's not wrong, though. My business has overtaken my life. Even when I have time off, I'm usually just trying to decompress. I'm rarely on the prowl for someone to take home. I'm not in my twenties anymore, and honestly, it just sounds exhausting.

My last long-term relationship ended in disaster when my then-girlfriend didn't like how much I worked yet wanted to have higher limits on my credit cards that she used to shop with. When I told her those two things were mutually exclusive, she got mad and cheated on me with some muscled-up bodybuilder.

Great. Now, I'm in a bad mood from just the thought of that selfish bitch.

Allison starts talking about something that I'm only half paying attention to, and apparently, she can tell.

"Aiden, are you even listening to me?"

"Yeah, sorry."

"Just promise me something."

I'm hesitant to agree to anything she asks me to promise her, but I'm about over this conversation.

"What?" I ask.

"Just for once in your life, let loose and have some fun. Romy is going to be stuck with you for an entire week. Don't be your typical grumpy self. Make it fun for her."

"I'm not grumpy," I argue.

"Yeah, sure. And I love dick."

"Allison! Gross!" I cry.

"I said I *don't* like it. I was being sarcastic," she groans.

"I still don't like hearing my sister saying the word *dick*."

"Promise me, Aiden, and I won't say it anymore."

I know she's probably full of shit, but I'm ready to end this conversation, so I promise anyway and hang up the phone.

After I hit the END button, my eyes flick up, and I see Romy doing a little jog out to her car. She's bundled up in her oversized coat, looking like an Eskimo.

She roots around in her old beat-up car for a moment before reappearing, holding her phone charger.

She heads back inside but drops the little white cord on the way. I watch her struggle to bend over and pick it back up with her mittens still on. It takes her a minute to finally grab it. When she does, she quickly shuffles back inside.

Romy isn't quite cut out for Minnesota winters. Maybe this trip to Florida will do her some good. Hell, maybe it'll help me to thaw out too—in the metaphorical sense anyway. I'm basically a grizzly bear, so the cold doesn't bother me.

Watching Romy run back inside, shivering the whole way, I made two crucial decisions.

One, I'm going to listen to Allison and try to relax and let loose a little on this trip.

And two, I *really* need to get Romy a space heater.

# Chapter Three

## ROMY

"So, you're going on a week-long vacation with your boss?" My best friend, Veronica, asks me. She's sitting on my bed, fiddling with her bright red hair. She's had it dyed that color for as long as I can remember.

"V, it's not a *vacation.* It's some construction conference thing. I'm sure it's going to be all work and no play," I say.

"Romy, you're going to be in Key West. Construction conference or not, I'm sure you're going to have some fun. Didn't you say that your boss is a hottie?"

"I most certainly never said that!" I exclaim.

"Well, *is he?*" Her eyes are as big as saucers.

"I mean, he's attractive in a mountain man sort of way, I guess. But he's always wearing a baseball cap and multiple layers of clothing, so it's not like I can see all that much. And even if I *could,* I *shouldn't.* He's my boss, for God's sake." I pull some more clothes out of the closet and set them on the bed to be packed.

"What happened to you?" Veronica asks. "Back in college, you were way more fun. You'd be trying to climb that man like a tree without any fear of the consequences."

"Back in college, things were different, and you know it."

She simply nods because she knows *exactly* what changed. In a heartbeat, I went from being a well-off trust fund babe who cared more about partying than school to losing every cent I had and hoping my grades were enough to get me through, so I could graduate and get a good job.

Ever since, I've worked hard for everything I have. That's why I can't do anything to ruin this job.

I just can't.

I know Veronica probably wouldn't understand that, though. The woman runs entirely on impulse and pheromones.

"Do you think he finds you attractive?" She asks.

"I highly doubt it. I'm pretty sure I'm like his annoying work wife who is on his ass most of the time."

"I didn't ask about how he personally felt about you. I asked if you think he finds you attractive."

"Well, I doubt that too. Every day, I go to work bundled up like I'm trekking through the arctic. And every day, I wear my hair in the exact same messy bun with the same nerdy glasses. I don't exactly dress to impress."

She holds up one of the shirts I just packed. "Clearly, you have the same mindset for this trip too."

"What's wrong with that top?" My voice goes a couple of octaves higher than usual.

"It's just so...blah. Don't you have anything else more fun in that closet of yours?" Before waiting for my reply, she gets up and walks past me, examining all the clothes still hanging up.

Rapidly, she starts picking out things and draping the hangers over her arm. When she comes out, she sets the entire pile on the bed next to my suitcase.

There's a lot of sundresses in the pile, along with a cocktail dress, some jeans and tank tops, and a tiny string bikini.

"No way!" I exclaim. "I can't wear this stuff in front of my boss!"

"Who says?"

"I say! Not to mention the fact that I'm a good twenty pounds heavier than I was when I bought all this stuff."

Between stress-eating and my metabolism slowing with age, my body also went downhill with everything else during my college years. That's another big reason why my wardrobe consists more of loose-fitting items these days.

"Oh, please, Romy. Who cares if you have a little extra fluff? Most all of it went to your ass and your tits."

"And my stomach," I argue.

"Barely."

Now, don't misunderstand me. I don't think I'm hideous. There's nothing wrong with being a little curvy but seeing as I used to be pretty damn skinny, I just have some issues feeling comfortable in my own skin sometimes.

Back then, I barely had any boobs to speak of, and now, they're way more than a handful. Between their newly formed stretch marks and all of the eyes leering at them constantly, I usually feel more comfortable hiding them and pretending they don't exist.

Veronica just picked out all of the clothes that would have the girls on full display for the whole world to see.

No, thank you.

"Make sure you take your contacts too, so you don't have to wear your glasses the whole time," she says.

"What's wrong with my glasses? I need them to, you know, SEE!"

"That's also what contacts are for. And then, everyone can see your pretty blue eyes."

"You understand this is a work thing, right? I'm not going to make a love connection."

She busies herself with folding a shirt. "I know, but how about you have some fun too? Maybe you can find someone to at least give you an orgasm."

I scoff. "V, I have orgasms all the time."

Her eyes roll. "I'm talking about the kind of orgasms not brought on by your own fingers or a vibrator. When was the last time you had a man climb between your legs and settle in, ready to give you every type of pleasure imaginable? When was the last time a man made you come so hard your legs wouldn't stop shaking?"

"I don't remember," I lie. The truth is that I've never had a man do any of those things.

All of the men I let take me to bed in college were pretty self-obsessed and didn't care much beyond getting their dicks wet. Whether or not I had an orgasm wasn't even on their radar —let alone a mind-blowing one.

"Romy, all I'm saying is if the opportunity comes knocking, don't ignore it. Open the door, and let that bitch in."

I can't help but laugh at her dramatic attitude. And before I can change the subject, she throws her hand over her heart and adds, "Thank you for listening to this public service announcement from none other than your vagina."

*Oh, lord.*

# Chapter Four

## AIDEN

"Are you okay?" I ask Romy.

I feel awful because she's wedged between myself and another huge man who seems to be pretty wasted.

"I'm fine," she insists, but I don't believe her bravado.

I didn't realize her seat was in the middle when I bought our airline tickets. When we boarded, I immediately offered to switch her, but she insisted that this would be easier since she was smaller.

I don't think she expected Mr. Two Fisted Shots to be seated next to her.

I'm pretty sure this guy was drunk long before he stepped foot on this plane. The second he sat down, I could smell the alcohol seeping from his pores. I should have known then and there that this guy was going to make an ass out of himself.

I keep watching him out of the corner of my eyes, and he's eyeing Romy like he's undressing her in his mind. When the flight attendant comes over to give him the drink he just ordered, his arm reaches across Romy and intentionally grazes her breast.

White-hot rage courses through my veins as I fight every impulse I have to knock this guy's head off his fucking shoulders. My fingers wrap around the armrest so hard my knuckles turn white.

Romy's eyes meet mine, and she silently mouths, "It's fine."

*No, the fuck it's not.*

I try my hardest just to let it go, but when he sets his hand on her thigh and burps in her face before saying, "How about you and I go get a drink when we get out of this tin can?"

*That's it.*

I'm about to tell him I think he's had more than enough to drink, but somehow, I don't think that would help. He'd probably just start a fight, and after I beat his ass, I'd likely be arrested once we landed.

Instead, I take a different approach.

Taking Romy's hand in mine, I link my fingers with hers and pray she doesn't pull away in horror.

She looks at me when I touch her, so I say, "So, baby, what do you want to do when we land?"

Her eyes go wide, but when I give her a subtle wink, she seems to catch on.

"Uhm…I don't know, *babe.* What do you want to do?" She asks, trying to play it cool.

I'm not sure if the guy is buying it because his hand is still firmly on her thigh.

Leaning over, I speak in a voice low enough for the two of them to hear but no one else. "Well, I know you wanted to hit the beach, but first, I want to stop by the room. I'm going to make you scream my name for a while before we go swimming. You know I can't keep my hands off you for very long."

She licks her lips as her chest heaves up and down at my words. It takes her a minute, but finally, she says, "Can't wait, baby."

The good news is that the creeper finally moved his hand and turned back to looking out the window.

The bad news is that I'm pretty positive Romy is completely freaked out. She's probably going to sue me for sexual harassment.

She seems to go with the flow, though, as she moves a little closer to me, leaning her head on my shoulder. She gets comfortable and starts to doze off.

And to my amazement, she stays there the rest of the flight.

When we finally land, I wake her up, and she looks utterly mortified.

"I'm sorry," she whispers.

"Not a problem," I assure her. "Let's just get out of here."

Once we are off the plane, we grab our luggage and head over to get our rental car. The whole time, we are pretty quiet, as if neither of us has a clue of what to say.

It isn't until we are finally in the car on our way to the resort that either one of us finally speaks.

I start the conversation off. "Hey, I'm sorry about that thing on the plane. I didn't know how else to get that jerk to leave you alone, aside from beating him to a pulp. And I try not to fight if I can help it."

She looks confused. "Why are you sorry? You got that creep to leave me alone, and then, you didn't even complain when I slept on you for half the flight. I should be thanking you."

"I just didn't want to make things weird or anything."

She gives me a casual smile. "Not weird at all. I promise."

I don't know if I entirely believe her, but I decide just to let it go for fear of making things even more awkward.

I look over at her in her long sleeve shirt and sweatpants and can't help but chuckle a little.

Looking embarrassed, she asks, "What?"

Glancing down at my own outfit, I reply, "Just thinking about how you and I are both going to have to rethink our wardrobes to acclimate to this warmer weather."

"True," she laughs. "It'll be nice not to have to wear my giant winter coat."

When I look over at her, she's smiling ear to ear. I've never noticed how cute it is until now. I guess my typical grumpy disposition doesn't give her much of a reason to smile at work.

As we pull up to the resort, I hand the keys to the valet, and I grab our bags out of the back. Romy reaches for hers, but I tell her I've got it.

I give my name at the check-in desk, and the man pulls out two room keys and hands one to each of us.

"Rooms 2102 and 2103, sir. The rooms are adjoining," he says.

Romy looks a little uncomfortable, so I try to put her at ease.

"There weren't a lot of room choices since I booked so late. Don't worry; I'll only use the front door." I shoot her a wink.

She returns a warm smile.

When we are outside of our rooms, I say, "How about we go get settled and change clothes, and we can grab some dinner? This resort has a couple of great restaurants. One is a steak-house, I think."

"Sounds great," she agrees.

We set a time and head inside our separate rooms. It's been a hell of a day so far, and I'm wondering if the rest of the week will be equally as eventful.

# Chapter Five

## ROMY

The moment I shut my hotel room door, I lean against it and let out the breath I feel like I've been holding for hours.

*What the fuck happened on that plane?*

Now, I'm not complaining about Mr. Montgomery saving me from the creep next to me. That was very knight-in-shining-armor of him.

What I can't seem to figure out is why when he touched my hand, I got butterflies. And why when he talked about making me scream his name, I got oddly excited at the thought.

Maybe Veronica was right—it's been too long since I've had contact with a male. So long that the thought of bedding my boss is actually running through my mind.

Deciding I need to try to clear my mind, I head in to take a shower. After I turn on the hot water, I take a moment to admire the luxurious bathroom with the spacious walk-in shower and oversized garden bathtub. The decor is ocean-themed, and the tile and countertops appear to be marble.

After my hot shower, I finally take a moment to look at the room itself. It's got a king-sized bed across from a dresser with a large TV on top of it. On one end of the room, there's a little kitchenette with a small table, and on the other, there are two large red curtains that cover almost the whole wall.

When I walk over to pull them back, I gasp at the sight. On the other side of the large sliding glass doors, I have the most fantastic view of the beach right below me and the crystal blue water of the ocean.

I'm mesmerized watching the small waves crash onto the white sand beach.

I open the glass door and step out onto the balcony. There are a couple of chairs, so I take a seat on one. The warm air wraps around my skin while the salty smell fills my nose. This is the epitome of what paradise must be. Watching the waves is entrancing.

I have no idea how long I sit out there, but when my freshly washed hair is almost completely dry, I figure it's time to head inside. It'll be time for dinner soon.

Once I'm inside, I open my suitcase and start pulling things out, looking for something to wear. There's just one problem.

Almost every item that I pull out isn't something that I packed. How the hell did all of this stuff get in here?

*Veronica.*

That bitch didn't need to use the bathroom. She walked back to my room and repacked my whole fucking suitcase!

Now, all that is in here is dresses, jean shorts, tank tops, and a couple of pairs of jeans that I'm not even sure fit me anymore. Oh, and that tiny-ass bikini.

*What the hell am I supposed to wear?*

Pulling out my phone, I type the words. **YOU'RE DEAD** in a text message and fire it off to Veronica.

I'm even more annoyed when she responds with:

**New number. Who dis?**

When I don't respond, she changes her tone in her following message.

**I'm sorry. Just please try to have some fun. Your vagina will thank you.**

I turn my phone on silent to not be distracted while trying to find something halfway decent to wear.

Finally, I decide on a pair of jeans (which somehow miraculously fit) and a black sparkly tank top. This will work for tonight, but I'm going to have to work some miracles for the rest of the week.

And of course, all I have in the undergarment department is push-up bras and thongs. And when I say thongs, I mean *thongs.* You know the type that is like floss in the back and just doesn't quite seem to ever cover your entire vagina?

Speaking of which, why is that such a novel concept? If I'm a bigger girl looking to hide some panty lines and buy a bigger thong, I expect it to cover my whole vajayjay.

But I guess I'm just going to have to live with a half-covered pussy.

Awesome.

Glancing at the clock, I realize I'm running out of time, so I quickly get dressed and head back into the bathroom. Looking in the mirror, I figure I may also do this up right, so I switch my glasses out for my contacts and use my curling wand to add a few waves to my hair.

After a coat of mascara and some lip gloss, I'm out the door.

When I get downstairs, I head inside the restaurant. Walking up to the host station, I ask if Mr. Montgomery has arrived yet. When they say no, they go ahead and seat me at an empty table.

When the server comes over, I order a rum and Coke along with a water.

I look down at my phone and see a text from Mr. Montgomery.

**Headed down now. I'll get us a table.**

I text back saying I already got us one and let him know about where in the restaurant I'm seated.

Fidgeting in my seat, I try to pull my hair in front of my shoulders, hoping maybe it hides my ample cleavage that is trying to pop out and say hello.

Trying to sit still, I take a sip of my drink, but when my

eyes flick up, I choke on it at what I see.

A man is walking toward me, but it's not just any man. It's a man who looks like he belongs on the cover of a romance novel —a dirty one. A man who looks like he could have every woman in the room on her knees in a heartbeat.

A man who just happens to be my boss.

That's right. Walking toward me is none other than Mr. Montgomery.

But holy hell, he looks different.

That hair that is always hidden under a hat? Now, there's no hat, and his hair is longer than I ever would have guessed— like halfway down his back long. It's dark brown, almost black, and straight and shiny.

His neatly trimmed beard matches, and his hand scratches it as he walks toward me.

His typical layers of clothing have been replaced with some form-fitting dark blue jeans and a black button-down shirt. The top few buttons are undone, showing off his dark chest hair. The sleeves are rolled up to just below the elbows, and I can see the veins roping down his forearms.

His body doesn't look like that of a bodybuilder. Instead, he's burly and stocky. And I find myself wondering what he looks like under that clothing.

*Stop that.*

"Hey, Romy," he greets with a smile.

Clearing my throat, I respond, "Hi, Mr. Montgomery."

He sits down across from me, and immediately, our server is upon us.

He orders a whiskey before turning his attention back to me.

"Romy, you and I are going to be here for an entire week with each other. How about you call me Aiden?"

"Aiden," I say the name, feeling how it sounds on my tongue. "Okay, then."

The waitress brings back his drink, but we tell her we need more time to look over the menu. We peruse all of the choices, and he decides on a surf 'n turf while I settle on a fried seafood platter. After we order, he looks back at me.

But he's not staring at my overly-exposed boobs. No, his light caramel-colored eyes are staring directly into mine.

I'm not sure exactly what to say, and as usual, I proceed to stick my foot in my mouth. "You look different. I mean, not bad different. You look good—really good." My mouth snaps shut, and my face turns beet red.

*Why do I have to be so damn awkward?*

But Aiden just chuckles. "Thank you. Usually, at work, I dress for convenience and comfort rather than style. But I figure we are on vacation—well, kind of—so I might as well let my hair down—so to speak."

"Well, the warm climate looks good on you."

"Back at you, Romy. You look amazing. Is that weird of me to say?" He asks. "Did I make things uncomfortable?"

I smile. "Not any more than I already have."

Changing the subject, he asks, "Are you enjoying the warm climate? Finally starting to thaw?"

"Yes!" I sip my drink. "Thank goodness. Earlier, I just sat on my balcony watching the waves. I could have sat there for hours."

He gives a slight laugh. "Funny. I did the same thing. It's been forever since I've been at a beach."

"I've never been."

His eyes go wide. "Never?"

I shake my head. "Nope. The only time I ever left Minnesota was to go to college in Arizona, which is really one big desert."

"Nothing wrong with that. I'm just a little surprised."

My brow furrows. "Why?"

"Every day, I watch you bundle yourself up like a cute little Eskimo and freeze your ass off dealing with the harsh Minnesota weather. I figured you would have traveled South by now."

"Minnesota is my home," I begin. "As much as I hate the cold, I would feel weird leaving. Plus, that would mean leaving my boss, and I'm pretty sure he'd fall apart without me," I tease.

'You're probably right." He smiles for a moment before his expression turns serious again. "For what it's worth, Romy, I am damn lucky to have you. You do so much for this company and me. I know I don't say it nearly enough, but you are so appreciated."

"I'm just doing my job," I mutter.

"No, Romy, don't sell yourself short. I need to do better at showing you your value. Because you really are amazing."

The way he looks at me makes me *feel* his words, but there's something I can't quite put my finger on.

There is one thing I am sure about, though—I'm in so much fucking trouble.

# Chapter Six

## AIDEN

Romy might have said I looked good, but she looks fucking stunning. Getting away from Minnesota does wonders for her.

I never realized how long her hair is. Of course, she's probably thinking the same thing about me. At work, I always wear my hair under my hat. It keeps it out of my way while I get shit done.

And now, she's wearing contacts which makes it easier to see her pretty blue eyes.

And the outfit she's wearing? Holy fuck. I'm struggling not to let my eyes drift down to her low-cut shirt. Usually, she wears baggy clothing, so I had no idea what was hiding underneath.

It doesn't take long for our food to show up, and we dig in. I offer her part of my lobster, and it doesn't take much to convince her to take it.

"This is delicious," she says between bites.

I nod and get the server's attention to order us each another drink.

Once they appear, I take a sip and ask, "So, tell me about college in Arizona." I remember on her resume that she had a degree in business and finance, but that's all I know.

"Hot," she responds with a smile.

Jokingly, I say, "You really have a thing about weather,

don't you? You're either too hot or too cold."

She giggles. "Here in Florida, it feels just right."

"Okay, Goldilocks. Anything else memorable about college?"

She twists the straw around the rim of her glass. "Well, I lived on campus with a girl named Veronica. We're still best friends to this day. V is a bit of a free spirit, so she moved back to Minnesota with me when she graduated."

"That's awesome. It seems like most people get more horror stories from their college roommates rather than a best friend."

"I definitely got lucky." She smiles, thinking about her friend. "Of course, sometimes I want to kill her. When we got here, I realized she'd repacked my entire suitcase. Hence the crazy outfit." She looks down at herself and sighs.

I'm not sure exactly what to say without sounding like a total pervert. I settle on, "Well, for what it's worth, I think you look great—no matter what you're wearing."

*Nope. Still creepy.*

But she just gives me a warm smile. "Thank you."

"So, did you do a lot of partying back in your college days?" I ask.

Her body tenses slightly as though I've touched a nerve. "For a while, but after a big dose of reality, I buckled down and focused on studying."

I'm curious to know about that 'big dose of reality', but I don't want to make her feel uncomfortable, so I don't ask.

Turning the spotlight away from herself, she asks, "What about you? Where did you go to college?"

"I didn't. Well, not in the literal sense anyway. I went to a trade school in town. I worked during the day to get on-the-job training and took all of the classroom stuff in the evenings."

She nods. "Sounds exhausting."

I chuckle. "It was, but I made it through and didn't have any debt when I was done with it all."

"Lucky you. How long did it take you to start your own

business?"

"A few years," I begin. "This is going to sound super lame of me, but I lived with my parents while I was in college and a few years after so I could save up every cent that I made. No one wanted to give me a loan, so I had to start small and fund it myself for a while."

"I don't think that sounds lame at all. I think it's pretty damn impressive that you've built such a thriving business in such a short time."

Hearing her praise me gives me a proud feeling, but I'm not quite sure why. Hell, I got asked here to give a speech about my accomplishments, and I didn't feel as happy as I do right now listening to Romy hype me up.

We continue to talk, even long after we finish our food. We just keep ordering drinks and shootin' the shit.

When our waitress keeps giving us dirty looks for hogging her table, I ask Romy if she wants to take a walk. She agrees, so I order us another round and pay the check, leaving a hefty tip.

Once we leave the restaurant, we walk through the resort's lobby and out the back doors. We walk past the pool and the hot tub along a cobblestone path that leads straight to the beach.

When we reach the sand, she kicks off her shoes and bends over to pick them up. She looks a bit wobbly when she stands back up, so I put my hand on her arm to steady her.

She laughs. "Guess it's been a while since I've had this much to drink."

"That's alright. I've got you," I say, still holding onto her.

She chuckles to herself.

"Something funny?" I ask.

"Just thinking about how you're not nearly as grumpy as you are at work."

That gets a full-fledged belly laugh out of me. "Yeah, I know I come off as grumpy most of the time. I guess when I'm at work, I'm just so focused on it that I don't think about much else. I know it's something I need to work on. My sister reminds me of that constantly."

"You have a sister?" She asks.

I nod. "A twin. Allison. She's older than me by two minutes, and she never lets me forget it."

"Oh, Allison is your sister," she says the words as though a light bulb just switched on.

"Yeah…"

She smiles. "It just makes sense now as to why you ask me to send flowers to a woman named Allison every year on your birthday."

Not only am I surprised that she remembers when my birthday is, but I'm also shocked she spent any time wondering who the flowers were for.

"Do I detect a hint of jealousy?" I tease.

Getting embarrassed, she stammers, "What? No! Maybe a little curious. I mean, who sends flowers to someone else on their own birthday. It was just odd—"

I cut her off. "Romy, I'm just giving you a hard time."

Her cheeks turn pink in the most adorable way. "Oh, right." she pauses a moment before asking, "So, I sent flowers to your sister, but never anyone else. Does that mean no girlfriend?"

I smile. "Nope. No girlfriend."

"Is there something wrong with you?"

I pull my hair back to get it off my neck and secure it with the rubber band around my wrist. "Oh, where to begin? I work too much. Typically, when I get home, I'm too exhausted to want to go out and do anything. I don't have some perfect chiseled body. And you know, I'm sort of grumpy."

"You're not so bad," she says with a smile. "Besides, after some of the jerks I've dated, I'd think it'd be nice to have someone who is actually on the right path—someone with goals and ambition."

I shrug. "I mean, I get it. As I said, I tend to have tunnel vision when it comes to working. The last woman I was dating seriously was Jane, and maybe I took her for granted at times. That is on me. Of course, it's on her for cheating on me with her trainer."

"Ouch."

"It is what it is. After I caught her, she tried turning it back around on me, telling me she wished I would get in better shape because she wasn't into the whole 'dad bod' thing—her words, not mine."

She shakes her head. "That's still shitty. Back in the day, I dated a couple of gym rats. Did they look good? Sure. But they cared more about spending time in the gym than with me. And if I gained even a pound, they noticed. Back then, I was quite a bit skinnier." She looks down at herself.

"Not to sound weird, but I think you look great. I prefer a woman with curves and some meat on her. It's more fun to have something to hold onto."

*Oh lord, I can't believe I just said that. Maybe I've had too much to drink too.*

But she doesn't seem to be offended. Instead, she says, "I'm sure glad you said that because I've wanted to do this for a while."

With one hand, she reaches down and undoes the button on her jeans.

Sighing in relief, she says, "Sorry. I haven't worn these jeans in forever, and they're a little small. After dinner, I felt like I couldn't breathe."

"Don't feel like you have to explain yourself. You should be comfortable."

We walk a little further down the beach, and I can't help but notice how beautiful she looks in the moonlight. I feel like such a jerk that I've never really noticed before. Romy has always just been my assistant—my mousy assistant who isn't afraid to give me her input or call me on my bullshit when needed.

And here I am, making the same mistakes I always have. I'm not appreciating a good woman who is right in front of me. It might be in a different way than it was with Jane, but the principle remains the same.

But no more. From here on out, I will make sure I don't

take Romy for granted any longer.

# Chapter Seven

## ROMY

My head is fuzzy from all the alcohol I've had, but there's one thing I'm sure of.

Everything I thought about Aiden is proving to be completely false. He's not just some gruff asshole who only cares about his work.

I would never have guessed that he's actually charming, sincere, and funny. And did I mention attractive? Because damn.

And I feel oddly comfortable around him. I mean, yeah, we've worked together for three years now but have never had any interaction outside the typical 9-5. There should be no logical reason I, Miss Awkward and Weird, should feel so at ease around this man.

But here we are. Maybe the alcohol is the thing pushing this along.

We talk about the conference for a little while, each discussing the different classes and seminars we want to attend. There's only one or two that we have in common—which is probably a good thing since I doubt I could concentrate for very long with Aiden sitting next to me.

"It's gorgeous out here," I say, stopping to look out over the waves.

"Yeah, it is," he replies. "One day this week, we will have to come out here and swim."

Feeling bold, I roll up the bottom of my pant legs and walk over to the water's edge. Slowly, I let the cool water touch my feet as the small waves crash against my ankles.

"Is it cold?" Aiden asks.

"A little." I shrug. "Why don't you come out here and see for yourself?"

"Nah, I'm good. This time of night is when the sharks come up to feed."

"What?!" I gasp and take off out of the water like I've been shot.

When I reach him, I practically climb up his body. And when he busts out laughing, I get the feeling he was probably joking.

"Are you fucking with me?" I ask.

Through his deep laugh, he answers, "Well, I'm pretty sure that's true, but I doubt they'd swim in water that only goes up to your ankles. And if they did, we'd probably see them."

"Not funny," I scold and playfully smack him on the chest. "I've got a decent amount of meat on this body. I'd make a great fatty meal for a shark and his buddies."

"You and me both."

I shake my head back and forth. "I'm sure you'd be too tough to eat. You're so tense all the time that it'd probably just be like eating gristle."

He laughs. "Oh, is that right?"

"Hey, I just call 'em like I see 'em," I joke.

We keep walking, and a comfortable silence falls between us for a few minutes.

The first one to speak again is me. "Don't you find this whole thing weird?"

Confused, he asks, "What whole thing?"

"You and I have worked together for three years now, and we barely know anything about each other. I've learned more about you today than I did in all those years. It's just crazy that you can know someone and not really *know* them."

"That's true. But I also think you and I already know more

about each other than you realize. Well, at least some of the important stuff."

"Oh, yeah?" My eyebrows raise. "What do you already know about me?"

He rubs his hand along the scruff of his beard. "Well, I know you have a good work ethic. You take pride in the work you do—no matter what that may entail. That's obvious by how organized you keep your desk. And you come to work even when you know you're going to freeze your ass off."

"What else?" I ask curiously because so far, he's not wrong.

"You're kind. No matter what, you treat everyone with sincere respect—until they do something that deems them unworthy of that respect. Then, you take no shit.

"And you're caring. Caring enough to keep your grumpy boss organized and keep the business running smoothly."

I don't know how, but somehow this man is saying everything I need to hear him say. Under that tough exterior is a really sweet guy. And maybe it's his kind words. Maybe it's the alcohol. Maybe it's both.

But my head is swimming. I'm not quite sure what's happening, and I'm one hundred percent sure I'll regret this in the morning, but at this moment, I don't care.

I stop walking, and he turns toward me to make sure I'm okay.

Looking up at him, I stare into his caramel eyes. The moon lights them up enough to still see the beautiful color.

Quietly, I say, "Don't fire me for this, okay?"

Leaning up on my tiptoes, I press my lips against Aiden's. In my typical fashion, it's a bit clumsy and awkward.

When he pulls back to look at me, I fear I've made a colossal mistake, but when my eyes meet his once more, I see something that wasn't there before.

Lust.

His large hands grab each side of my face and pull me back in. This time, when our lips touch, there's nothing awkward about it.

His lips massage mine, and I feel his tongue run along the seam of my mouth, seeking entrance. I open for him, and as his tongue finds mine, heat spreads throughout my body.

Good lord, the man can kiss.

One hand moves from the side of my face down to my waist. It tugs me even closer, so our bodies are firmly pressed together. His large frame feels so warm against mine.

My hands fist in the material of his shirt, attempting to hold onto something—anything—that will keep us locked in this moment forever. Right now, it doesn't matter that he's my boss. All that matters is that we can't get enough of each other.

I have no idea how long we stand there just making out like a couple of teenagers. (No, fuck that. No teenager can kiss this well.). The only thing that finally breaks us apart is hearing some other people come walking down the beach.

Aiden looks down at me as if waiting for me to decide what I want to happen from here. Now would be a perfect opportunity for me to call it a night—to tell him we shouldn't go any further and should just go back to our rooms.

Yes, that would be the smart thing to do...

But maybe I'm just an idiot because that's literally the *last* thing I want to do.

"Do you want to go up to my room?" I whisper breathlessly.

In response, he gives me the sexiest smile I've ever seen. If my panties weren't wet before, they sure are now.

He takes my hand and leads me back inside. It feels like the longest walk of my life. In the lobby, I press the button for the elevator, and we wait impatiently.

The doors finally open, and a couple of people step out as we step in. The moment the doors close behind us, it's as though any sliver of self-control we have goes right out the window.

Aiden's mouth crashes down on mine once again. One hand fists in my hair while the other palms my ass cheek. I squeal when he gives it a quick smack.

The ride to our floor is a fast one, and when the doors open once again, he leads me down the hall, stopping just in front of my door. Pulling the key out of my back pocket, I unlock it, and we head inside.

Once again, the moment that door closes, we are pulled to one another by some invisible force. Aiden pushes me up against the door, pinning my arms above my head while his kisses start at my mouth and slowly work their way down my neck and collarbone.

I let out a loud moan as he softly nips the top of my cleavage. He gets on his knees in front of me, making his face perfectly aligned with my chest. His rough hands move under my shirt, holding onto my sides. When his fingers grab the hem of the sparkly material, they pull it off over my head.

Usually, I'd be super self-conscious about my poochy belly and love handles, but right now, I couldn't care less. And the way Aiden is looking at me tells me he doesn't care either.

I don't even mind when he pulls my jeans down, exposing my barely-there thong. I'm honestly surprised my vagina hasn't swallowed it by now.

Once they're off, his eyes look me up and down from the skimpy material of the underwear to the lacy fabric of my push-up bra.

"Fucking beautiful," he says in a low tone. And the way he says it makes me believe him.

He trails kisses along my chest while his fingers expertly unhook the clasp of the bra. Once he pulls it down my arms and off my body, his hands get to work, lifting one in each hand and grazing my nipples with his thumbs. When his warm mouth replaces his thumbs on the sensitive flesh, I cry out. The sensation of his tongue flicking against the pink nubs pulls an invisible string that's attached directly to my clit.

My legs press together in an attempt to quell the ache forming between them. Aiden must sense what I am craving because his fingers move aside the thin fabric of my thong and start sliding through the wet folds. He focuses his attention on my clit, rubbing small circles around the bundle of nerves.

When he takes a finger and slips it inside, I let out another loud moan. Oh, who am I kidding? I've been noisy as hell this whole time.

Once inside, he presses against my g-spot, sending sparks of electricity shooting through me like fireworks.

Without warning, he hooks one of my legs over his shoulder and sinks down further, giving his mouth perfect access to my pussy. And holy hell, what the man does with that access is nothing short of amazing.

He doesn't just eat my pussy.

He *devours it.*

His tongue licks every inch of me, lapping up all my juices. His arms snake around my waist, holding me in place since my legs are starting to quiver.

It feels so damn good that I never want it to end, but I'm heading toward my orgasm at lightning speed. When he gently sucks my clit between his teeth and uses his tongue to flick against the most sensitive part, my resolve breaks, and I'm coming undone.

My entire body quakes as I struggle to stay upright— seemingly endless waves of pleasure wash over me. I scream out Aiden's name in a voice I barely recognize as my own.

Once my body stills, he slowly sets my leg back on the ground. When he looks up at me, the lust in his eyes shows that we are far from done.

He gets up off his knees and looks me up and down again. With one firm command, he has my knees going weak once more.

"Get on the bed."

# Chapter Eight

## AIDEN

I am going straight to hell. Do not pass Go. Do not collect two hundred dollars.

I just made my assistant come all over my face.

Should I feel weird about that?

*Probably.*

*Do* I feel weird about that?

*Fuck, no.*

Watching Romy come might be the hottest thing I've ever seen.

Never mind, the sight of her naked, lying on a bed waiting for me, is the hottest thing I've ever seen.

The moment she laid down, I wasted no time in removing the tiny thong, so now, she's wearing nothing at all.

Her curvy body looks so soft and beautiful.

Not wanting to wait any longer, I unbutton my shirt and yank it off. I may not be the most attractive guy. I may not have a chiseled body or perfect six-pack abs, but I'll make damn sure she doesn't forget this night. I'll make sure she has as many orgasms as she can handle.

Before I take off my jeans, I pull the condom out of my wallet and toss it on the bed in front of me. I call it my 'just in case' condom. At this point, I'm not even entirely sure how long it's been in there.

But right now, I don't care. An old condom is better than no condom at all.

Unzipping my pants, I pull them and my plaid boxers off, causing my cock to spring free. I stroke it up and down a few times before grabbing the rubber. As I roll it on, I catch the look on Romy's face. She is propped up on her elbows, gazing at what my hands are doing.

When it comes to length, I'm about average, but girth is where I stand out. I guess it's thick, just like the rest of me is.

My knees hit the bed, causing the mattress to sink as I make my way between her legs. She spreads them for me, giving me the perfect view of her glistening pussy.

I climb on top of her and kiss her slowly and deeply. She melts into me and wraps her arms around my neck.

When I feel her hips lift and arch toward me, I know she's ready.

Reaching between us, I position myself at her entrance. As I begin to push in, I never stop kissing her. She moans into my kiss as she feels me stretch her. I go slowly to give her time to adjust, but once I'm fully inside, she pulls back from our kiss and looks up at me.

In a sultry whisper, she says, "Fuck me, Aiden."

If I had even the tiniest scrap of self-control before, it all just went out the window. I've always preferred sex to be a bit on the rougher side—it just seems to make it more fun. But I wasn't going to do that with Romy. She looks like a beautiful, delicate flower, and I intended to treat her as such.

The look she's giving me, though, tells me that's not what she wants. So, I'll give her exactly what she asked for.

My hips begin to move faster, plunging into her harder and deeper. Every time she moans and cries out my name, it adds fuel to my fire.

I prop myself up on my knees and hold onto her legs for better leverage. With every thrust, her tits bounce up and down. Between that and the way she's biting her lip, I have the perfect view.

Angling her legs on my shoulders, my hands grip her hips as I slam into her.

When she moans, "Oh, God!" I know she's close. I reach between her legs and rub her clit with the pad of my thumb. It's still sensitive from her earlier orgasm, so it doesn't take much to have her writhing beneath me. Her legs begin to shake on my shoulders as I continue fucking her through her orgasm.

Her pussy feels so fucking good. I want to stay like this and fuck her all night long, but the way she's clenching around my cock tells me that's not going to happen.

"Fuck, Romy," I growl through gritted teeth as I pump a few more times, filling the condom. Once our bodies still, I lean down and kiss her.

"Wow," she whispers.

"Yeah. No joke," I say with a laugh.

I stand up and head into the bathroom to throw away the rubber and splash some water on my face.

While in there, the enormity of what we just did hits me.

I just had sex with my assistant.

When my dick was hard, it was obvious why that didn't seem like a huge deal. I have a brain and a cock and enough blood to only run one of them at a time.

That doesn't explain why I'm not too freaked out about it right now. Maybe it's because Romy and I have always had such a good relationship—albeit a working one.

*Or maybe she's fucking amazing, and I'm so stupid that I'm just now realizing it.*

I will say that even before the sex, it's been a long time since I've ever had such a good time with someone. There was a certain ease and comfortability to it.

In this place, it doesn't feel like I'm her boss, and she's my assistant. It feels like something different. It feels like something *more*.

When I come out of the bathroom, I fully plan on talking to her about all of this. But as I walk out, she's still lying in bed and is now softly snoring.

Walking over to the bed, I slide in next to her and pull her close. Her hair smells like vanilla as I place a soft kiss on her shoulder.

"Sleep well, Romy," I whisper against her skin before I join her in a peaceful sleep.

# Chapter Nine

## ROMY

Slowly, my eyes open, and I try to figure out where I am—definitely not my bedroom.

*Oh right. Hotel room in Key West.*

As I roll over, I realize I'm naked.

*Why am I naked?*

*Oh, right. I slept with Aiden.*

My eyes shoot open as I sit straight up, clutching the blanket to my chest.

Holy shit, I had sex with my boss. And I was the one who made the first move. I practically begged him to fuck me. What was I thinking?

*I was thinking that he looked hot as hell, and I wondered what it would feel like to have him touch me.*

Fucking amazing. That's how it felt.

My mind wanders for a minute, thinking about how good he made me feel. That whole thing about me never having an Earth-shattering orgasm? I can't say that anymore. Aiden gave me two.

But how weird is this going to make things now? Am I going to think about his face in between my legs every time I see him? Am I going to think about how thick his dick is while we are trying to work together?

Is this weird for him too? Is that why he snuck out? The

other side of the bed looks messy, so I'm guessing he slept in here. Plus, I vaguely remember cuddling after the sex.

What am I thinking? Of course, this is weird for him. I'm his fucking assistant. The one time I'm not quite so awkward and actually have a little bit of game, and I use it on my boss.

*Way to go, Romy.*

I get up out of the bed and stretch. As I make my way to the bathroom, my vagina is undoubtedly well aware that Aiden was there last night. It's not painful—more like just a pleasant reminder of his big member with every step I take.

*Great. Now, I'll be thinking about him all day.*

When I get to the bathroom, I do my business and decide to take a quick shower before starting the day. I throw my hair up in a messy bun and let the hot water run over me.

Once I shave my legs and wash my body, I dry off and throw on one of the plush robes hanging on the wall.

Steam billows out of the bathroom as I make my way back to the bed.

I about jump out of my skin when there's a knock at the door. Cracking it open, I see Aiden standing there with two to-go cups of coffee and a small white paper bag.

Stepping out of the way, I let him come in. "I thought you left," I say.

"Just to the lobby to grab us some breakfast. Oh, and I went to my room to grab a quick shower and a change of clothes." He sets the bag and one of the cups of coffee down in front of me, and I look him up and down.

Today, he's in another button-down shirt—this one, a dark gray, and his jeans are also a lighter color. His long hair is pulled back into a low ponytail, and he looks just as sexy as he did last night.

I clear my throat, attempting to get my mind out of the gutter. "I figured you were avoiding me."

"Why would I do that?" He asks, taking a seat across the table from me.

"Because of what happened last night," I say softly before

taking a sip of my coffee.

He takes a drink out of his own cup. "Oh, sweetheart, I wouldn't run from that. That was wonderful."

Goosebumps break out all over my skin, and I'm not sure if they are from Aiden calling me sweetheart or him also thinking it was wonderful.

"You don't think it was a mistake?"

"Not at all. Do you?"

I think for a moment. "No, but..."

He cuts me off. "Alright, Romy, here's how I see things—and feel free to stop me if I'm way off base here. You and I are both adults, and we seem always to be consumed with work. I don't know about you, but I don't have much of a social life when I go home at night, and I don't tend to make time for a lot of fun."

He pauses for a moment, so I say, "Yeah, me either."

"I know this is technically a work trip, but no one says we can't have some fun while we are here."

"Does that mean having sex again?" I ask with a small smile. I don't actually mean to smile, but the thought of it excites me.

Lord, I'm twisted.

His smile reflects back at me. "Well, I certainly wouldn't complain if we did. I had a lot of fun, but we don't have to if you're uncomfortable with it. I'm fine with just hanging out and trying to get to know each other better. Sex or not. It would be nice to just unwind for a week."

I can't help but think that having sex is a *perfect* way to unwind. And maybe that's the worst idea ever. I mean, is a week-long 'sex-cation' with my boss a great plan? Probably not. But it sounds like a shit ton of fun.

I think for a moment, trying to collect my thoughts. My eyes avoid looking at him, so his good looks do not sway me.

When I finally speak, I say, "Okay, here's what I'm thinking. You're probably right that both of us could probably use a break from all the stress. So, maybe we take this week and just have some fun—*all kinds of fun*—in the evenings. During the

41

day, we go to the conference and act like nothing more than colleagues. And at the end of the week, after we fly home, we go back to acting just like we always have."

He leans back in the chair, stretching his long legs in front of him. "I think that sounds like a good plan. But I meant it when I said if you want to keep things platonic, you just say the word. I'll never force you to do anything you don't want to do. And no matter what, your job is secure."

I smile. "I appreciate that. As far as I'm concerned, this week is just a free pass, and then things go back to normal. No harm, no foul."

He holds up the paper cup to toast. "Cheers to that."

# Chapter Ten

## AIDEN

This morning, Romy completely took me by surprise when she laid out her little preposition. I figured even though the sex was amazing, she would want to forget that it ever happened. After all, our judgments were both a little clouded last night.

So, the fact that she wants to keep this whole thing up for the next week was a pleasant surprise.

During the day, we took some different classes—mine focusing more on how to run a business and hers more on the administrative side of things. The material was interesting, but thoughts of Romy filled my head and clouded my thoughts. And I swear I could still smell the vanilla on her even though we were nowhere near each other.

Now, I'm waiting on her to finish up her last class. I watch everyone walking by. Most of them are burly construction guys. And a few are men you can tell are just check-writers—they own a business but have never actually gotten their hands dirty. Romy is definitely the best-looking person here, although she's completely unaware of that fact.

When she commented on how she had gained weight since college, I had two thoughts. One, who the hell *hasn't* gained weight since college? And two, someone must have made her feel bad about her curvier figure. Clearly, she just hasn't been with a man who truly knows how to handle those curves—until last night. And if she lets me, I'll show her over and over again all week long.

When Romy comes out of the large meeting room where her class was being held, I immediately notice her. She's wearing the same jeans from last night and an orange-sherbet-colored top that hangs off one of her shoulders. The shirt isn't low cut, but it also doesn't do anything to hide her ample chest. I try not to gawk because I'm sure men leering is why she usually tries to cover them up.

The moment her eyes find me, she smiles—a big warm, genuine smile. She walks past a string of men, all of whom stare at her like they'd love to watch those tits of hers bounce up and down while they're balls-deep inside her.

She doesn't seem to notice a single one of them, though. Or maybe she does notice and just doesn't pay them any mind. Instead, her eyes are focused entirely on me, and I fucking love it.

Still smiling, she greets me with a cheerful, "Hey."

My lips twist upward, unable to suppress my own grin. "Hey, you. How was your class?"

She rolls her eyes. "Pointless. Did you know that to be a successful administrative assistant, you should keep detailed records and make sure you have good organizational skills? I'm glad I took a class that stated the obvious," she says sarcastically.

A chuckle rumbles in my chest because I've never met a more organized and detail-oriented person than Romy. When I say she keeps my business in order and on track, I mean it. Still, she should be teaching a class on those subjects rather than taking one.

"I'm sorry it was lame," I say.

Her shoulders shrug. "It's alright. Hopefully, tomorrow's will be better."

"Or maybe you'll just be too smart for all of them, and you won't learn a damn thing."

"Probably," she quips. "But my boss brought me all the way

here, so I'll take the classes anyway."

We exchange a playful smile. "Oh, is that right?"

"Oh, yes," she jokes. "He runs a tight ship, and I better fall in line."

There's a sparkle in her eye when she looks up at me, so I lean in and, in a low tone, say, "I hope you are just as obedient later on."

I swear I hear her breath hitch in her throat, but she tries to play it off. Instead, she looks up at me once again and taunts, "What are you going to do if I don't obey?"

*Jesus, I'm about to fall apart.*

"Sweetheart, do you really want to find out?" I ask.

Her tongue flicks out and glides along her bottom lip. "Maybe I do."

Leaning even closer as we're walking, I say, "If you don't put that tongue back in your mouth, I'm going to be sporting a hard-on in front of all these people. And I'll have to pull you into one of these cleaning closets to take care of the problem."

Teasing me, she licks her lip again. "Don't threaten me with a good time."

She walks a few steps ahead of me, swaying her hips back and forth and putting on a bit of a show.

"Oh, you're going to pay for that later," I growl as I catch up to her. "Are you hungry?"

Her eyes narrow, causing a crease in her forehead. "Is that some sort of euphemism?"

I can't help but laugh. "Romy, if I was dirty talking, trust me, *I* would be the hungry one. And yes, I'm *very* hungry—I didn't get my fill last night. But first, how about we get some real food?"

Her skin blushes when I imply I'm hungry for her pussy, but she doesn't skip a beat. "Sounds good. I'm starving."

"Do you want to eat at the restaurant? I can go grab us a table."

She shakes her head. "Can we just go upstairs and order room service? I want to get out of these clothes."

Playfully, I joke, "Man, you really can't wait to get me naked, huh?"

Her jaw drops open as I start to walk away. "That's not…" she stammers. "That's not what I was implying."

When I sway my hips back and forth like she was just doing, she starts giggling.

"Anyone ever told you that you have a cute butt?" She asks.

"You should see it when I bend over," I tease, and she laughs even harder.

We step into the elevator to head upstairs. When the doors shut, I toss my room key on the ground.

"Oops," my hand playfully covers my mouth as I stick my backside out and bend over painfully slowly.

She laughs so hard that a cute snort comes out of her nose. It's fucking adorable.

"That's a prime piece of ass right there," she says, stepping closer to me and landing a quick smack to my ass.

I gasp and move my hips back and forth. I may look ridiculous, but it's worth it to hear Romy laugh.

She continues to slap my butt, and I shake it for her, and both of us are completely surprised when the elevator doors slide open before we get to our floor. An elderly couple stands there, and their eyes go wide at the sight before them.

Both of our faces fall, and I straighten up so fast I practically give myself whiplash. Romy and I both scoot to the corner as the appalled couple steps inside.

The tension in the big metal box is thick enough to cut with a knife. Romy and I both face the doors, trying to be as calm and relaxed as possible. But when I glance at her out of the corner of my eye, I see her mouth is pulled into a tight line, and her bottom lip quivers as she tries not to laugh.

As I watch her, it takes everything in me to keep a straight face.

The older gentleman keeps giving us uncomfortable side-eye that screams that he thinks we're total freaks.

Thankfully, the doors of the elevator open onto our floor a

few seconds later. We squeeze past the couple onto the patterned carpet of the hallway.

Once the doors slide shut behind us, we both keel over with the cries of laughter we've been holding in.

"Those people were mortified!" She exclaims.

Still laughing, we make our way back to her room. Once there, I hold the door open for Romy as she makes her way inside.

The moment the door closes behind me, I grab her arm and pull her back to me. My hands rest on either side of her face as my mouth finds hers. Her pillowy bottom lip feels so soft between mine.

Her body relaxes as she melts into me, wrapping her arms around my neck. The kiss goes on for a minute before I give her a couple of small pecks and pull back.

It takes a moment for her to open those blue eyes of hers to look at me.

Giving her a slight smile, I say, "Sorry. I've been thinking about doing that all damn day."

"Are you sure you're not some notorious ladies' man?" She asks, narrowing her eyes at me.

A laugh rumbles in my chest. "No, I don't think so. I get far less action than you think."

She purses her lips together like she doesn't believe me, but she doesn't press. Instead, she walks over to grab the room service menu.

"What sounds good?" She asks.

Walking toward her, I stand over her shoulder and look at all the options.

When I decide, I say, "How about a cheeseburger and fries?"

She turns her head and smiles up at me.

"Exactly what I was thinking."

Taking a seat on the bed, she picks up the phone. When they answer, she gives her room number and places the order. "Two cheeseburgers with fries and a six-pack of beer. Oh, and no onions or mayo on one of the burgers, please."

I'm cheesing like crazy when she hangs up. "You remember how I like my burger."

She seems unphased. "You're not the only one who pays attention to a lunch order, Boss Man. And for what it's worth, I also know that it isn't that you don't like onions—you're allergic to them."

My face contorts in confusion because I don't remember ever telling her that. I never make a huge deal out of it because it's not a super-serious allergy.

She notices the look on my face and says, "I pay attention, Aiden. My job is to keep you on track and organized. Part of that means making sure you don't eat something that would make you break out in hives."

She stands up and walks over to the window, and slides the large curtains open, bringing into sight the beautiful view of the ocean.

She stares out over the choppy water, and I stare at her. I've always known Romy was a great assistant—the best I could ask for. But it took me flying her a thousand miles away to see how truly remarkable she is. I feel like maybe I've been taking advantage of her all these years. When we get back, I think it's time to give her a raise.

A smile spreads across her lips, and a tiny giggle escapes.

"What's so funny?" I ask.

"Just thinking about the elevator."

When I start laughing too, she adds, "I never knew you were so funny. At work, you're so serious. I had no idea there was a big goofball underneath."

I shove my hands in my pockets and walk toward her. "Yeah, at work, I try to run a tight ship. In our line of work, deadlines are important, so I try to keep things on track. It doesn't always leave room for fun."

She shakes her head. "I get it. But I'm glad we're here now and that I get to see this side of you. I like this side."

"I'm glad too, Romy." Pulling her close, I wrap my arms

around her for a hug.

I *am* glad we are here together. And I'm happy we're letting loose and pushing past the boundaries of our relationship.

She and I have always been in sync—always had a strong connection, but this is different.

This is something I haven't felt in a very long time. It feels...real.

But we have a deal that this is only going to last a week and then end it. That's what Romy wants.

But I'll be damn sure it's a week she'll never forget.

# Chapter Eleven

## ROMY

"Here," I hand one of the fluffy white robes to Aiden. His large hand grabs it as he eyes it up and down. "Do I have to wear it?"

"Uh, yeah. Our deal was to eat room service in our robes?"

He nods. "I guess a deal's a deal. Besides, I guess a robe will be easier to take off you later."

When I look at him, there's a hunger in his eyes, and I'm about to say fuck the food and get down to the dirty stuff.

But my growling stomach makes its presence known right on cue.

Neither one of us mention it, but he asks, "Can I keep my underwear on? I don't know that a bellhop needs to see my one-eyed weasel."

I can't help but laugh. "One-eyed weasel? That's an...interesting name for it."

Stepping closer to me, he uses one finger to tilt my chin up to look at him. "How about after it fucks you again, you can come up with your own name for it?"

*Holy cow, this man is going to ruin my panties before he even touches me.*

Before I have any more time to picture climbing him like a tree, he walks away, pulling his shirt over his head.

When it slides off his body, I can see he has a large tattoo of a dragon that takes up most of his back. It's black and red and pretty intricate. I have no idea how I didn't notice it before.

Okay, that's not true. Last night, he had me in some sort of crazy sex haze. I wasn't paying any attention to what was on his back when I had those sexy eyes to look at...and his cock. I looked at that a lot too.

Trying not to drool all over myself thinking about his large member, I say, "Cool tattoo."

He looks over his shoulder toward his back as if forgetting about the giant artwork.

"Oh, thanks. I actually wish I wouldn't have gotten it."

"Why?" I ask. "It's beautiful."

He shrugs. "I got it when I was just out of high school—my form of rebellion or something."

"And you don't like it?"

"It's alright, but I wish I would have taken time to think more about what I wanted. Now, it's stuck on there forever."

"You could have it lasered off," I offer.

He lets out a heavy sigh. "True. But it would cost a ton and be painful as shit. Plus, it being there is like a constant reminder of how I shouldn't make stupid, reckless decisions."

"You don't think you sleeping with your assistant counts as stupid or reckless?"

He turns to me. "On the contrary." He places a teasingly soft kiss on my lips. "I think that might be the best decision I've ever made."

*Lord, he's good.*

He turns back away from me, taking off his jeans and slipping into the robe. He loosely ties it, so I can see the hair on his chest leading down his happy trail when he turns toward me.

Aiden might not have the six-pack abs that most women drool over, but his manly figure still screams sex appeal. He's the type of man you want to fuck you silly and then cuddle you all night long.

Realizing I'm staring, I blurt, "I don't have any tattoos."

"Trust me, I know. I took note of every part of your sexy

body last night. I would have noticed a tattoo."

"Right," I mutter.

"Why not? Can't decide what you want?"

Frantically, I shake my head back and forth. "I don't like pain. I'm a girl who cries when she stubs her toe. I'm not nearly enough of a masochist to put myself through getting drilled with a needle gun over and over again."

He laughs. "Fair enough."

Before either of us can utter another word, there's a knock on the door, signaling our food has arrived.

Aiden quickly walks over to answer it and signs the receipt before bringing our food inside. He rolls the small cart with the metal domes over to the table.

We take a moment to set everything up before we sit down to eat.

After I take my first bite, I nod. "Pretty good."

He follows suit and says, "Yeah, not bad, but I've had better."

"Agreed." I take another bite.

"So, Romy, tell me something about you."

"Like what?"

He takes a bite of a fry. "What's your favorite food besides those meatball subs you love so much?"

I point my finger at him. "Hey, don't hate on the all-mighty meatball sub. But aside from those, I love anything else that's Italian—spaghetti, lasagna, chicken parm. I love it all."

"Lucky for you, I make a mean lasagna."

"You cook?" My tone is laced with surprise.

"Don't sound so shocked. Yes, I cook. When I first started the business, money was pretty tight, so I asked my mom to teach me how. She showed me how to cook bigger meals, so I'd always have leftovers. I still don't eat out a whole lot."

Nodding, I reply, "Makes sense."

"Do you cook?"

I snort. "Do instant noodles and peanut butter and jelly sandwiches count?"

He laughs. "I don't think so."

"Yeah, you're probably right. I really should learn so I can make healthier stuff. I'm sure the extra pounds I've put on are from too many carbs and not enough salads." I don't say the words to elicit sympathy—more like I'm just stating a fact. Losing a few wouldn't be the worst thing in the world.

When I glance up, Aiden is staring at me. "You know, Romy, there's nothing wrong with not being a size two. Beautiful can look a lot of different ways. And for the record, I think you're beautiful."

My cheeks heat at the compliment. I can't remember the last time a man called me beautiful. I can't remember a time a man ever said it *period.*

Even back in my college days, when I was a bit more on the loose side, most guys I was with just called me hot or sexy—never beautiful.

Although I know what Aiden and I are is entirely temporary, there's a feeling in my gut that tells me I'm starting to have feelings.

Maybe it's just the excitement of it all—the newness.

Maybe not.

Maybe it's more.

But I keep telling myself it's the first one because maybe that way, I won't get hurt.

# Chapter Twelve

## AIDEN

I wonder if I've gone too far by telling Romy I think she's beautiful. I'm pretty sure I said it last night too, but I guess it takes a whole new meaning when you're not in the middle of having sex.

"You okay?" I ask when she hasn't spoken for a couple of minutes.

Her eyes slowly find mine. "I'm good. Just strange to hear myself called beautiful."

"Why?" It seems weird to me that no one would remind this woman daily how gorgeous she is.

Guilt hits me because up until yesterday, I'd never really noticed how lovely she is. She was always just my mousy assistant.

But here and now, I feel like the biggest idiot in the world for not noticing sooner.

And I'm her boss—I don't know that I'm supposed to notice. But I mean, the guys she's dated didn't call her beautiful?

"What kind of guys have you dated?" I ask. "None of them called you beautiful?"

A whisper of an embarrassed smile crosses her lips before she clears her throat to answer. "Most of the dating I've done has been more on the *casual* side. The couple of relationships that I could even begin to consider serious were with stupid frat guys who ended up cheating on me."

"Frat boys?" I smile. "That doesn't seem like your type."

"Yeah, you're telling me. I don't know what I was thinking."

"You were blinded by their abs and ability to drink beer out of a funnel," I joke.

She giggles. "You're probably right. There's nothing sexier than a man chugging beer so fast it comes out of his nose."

We both laugh at the thought before she says, "Back then, I was a pretty heavy partier, which seemed to attract the douche bags to me like bees to honey. The moment I got my shit together, they all ran the other way. I guess they'd rather have a girl who partied non-stop as opposed to one who spent all her free time studying."

It's hard for me to imagine Romy as the partying kind. She's so put-together—so organized. She doesn't seem like the type to lose it and let go of all her inhibitions.

When I tell her that, she chuckles. "Yeah, I've changed a lot. When life got rough, I got a big wake-up call. Let's just say I didn't like who I saw in the mirror, so I stepped up and made some changes."

This is the second time she's mentioned turning her life around because of some big event, but she still doesn't seem keen on talking about it, so I don't ask.

Instead, I decide to lighten the mood. When we are finished with our burgers, I say, "Okay, I have one critical question. I think the answer to it will determine whether or not we should go any further."

Her face slightly falls. "Okay, shoot."

"Star Trek or Star Wars?"

Any look of worry that was just written on her face a moment ago vanishes.

Her eyes narrow in on me, and her teeth sink into the corner of her lip as though she's mulling over her answer.

She lets out a loud sigh before saying, "Well, I hate to break it to you, Boss Man, but I'm a huge nerd. So, there's just no way to choose. I love them both."

"My God, you are the perfect woman, aren't you?" I ask.

Her nose crinkles when she smiles—like a damn adorable bunny or something. "I don't like to brag, but yes, I'm perfect," she teases.

That gets a loud laugh out of me. Romy is too damn cute for her own good.

She gives me a little wink before telling me she is going to brush her teeth. As she walks into the bathroom, I stand up to put our dishes back on the tray and roll everything back in the hallway.

After I finish, I walk past the bathroom door and catch a glimpse of my assistant. My legs stop moving, and I take a moment to take her all in.

*Oh yeah, I'm an idiot for not noticing before.*

She took her long hair out of the bun she had it in and is running her fingers through it.

Her robe slips down a little, showing off her shoulders and the top of her chest. Her skin is so soft and creamy.

Romy might have no idea, but her curves are *everything.*

I want to kiss every single inch of her. And instead of continuing to leer at her like a weirdo, I decide to do just that.

# Chapter Thirteen

## ROMY

I've just finished brushing out my hair when Aiden steps into the bathroom, positioning his large body behind mine.

He takes one hand and sweeps all of my hair to one side, exposing the skin on the back of my neck. His fingers lightly trace the sensitive flesh before replacing them with his mouth.

The moment the hairs from his beard graze against me, a shudder runs down my spine. Goosebumps break out across my body, and when he softly sinks his teeth into me, I let out a soft moan.

His hands grab the collar of the cotton robe and gently tugs it down my arms. He loosens the knot at the front, so it slides easily down my body.

The robe hits the floor, and my eyes avoid my naked body in the mirror. The only thing I have left on is my vagina-exposing thong. I really don't need to see how it doesn't cover me entirely or the way my stomach pouch hangs over the top of the material. Or how my breasts aren't quite as perky as they once were.

Between my cellulite and stretch marks, I have more body issues than I know what to do with.

I'm terrified to look at Aiden and see his reaction. After all, tonight, we aren't drunk. There's no alcohol haze to hide behind.

But when I get brave enough to look at his face, I see there's no disgust. It's quite the opposite. He is looking at me like I'm a fucking snack he wants to eat all night long.

His eyes move from my body to look at mine in the mirror. "Do you know how fucking sexy you are? Gorgeous," he whispers.

I shake my head back and forth.

"Allow me to show you," he says.

Still standing behind me, he wraps one hand around my neck. It's not rough or painful—more like possessive.

His other hand runs lightly across my skin, making me anxious for more. When his fingers find my nipple, I let out another moan—this one quite a bit louder. And when he rolls the hardening peak between his thumb and finger, I become putty in his arms. Moisture pools between my thighs at the slightest touch.

His hand travels from my neck down to my soaking panties. His fingers slip past the elastic of the thong and then through the thin patch of hair straight to my wet slit.

Two of his large fingers take their time rubbing me up and down, stroking my clit and making my knees go weak.

My head falls back against Aiden's chest—my eyelids heavy with lust.

But Aiden's gruff voice commands, "Romy, look in the mirror. Watch what I'm doing to this pretty pussy of yours. Look at how sexy you are."

My eyes drift back to the mirror, but this time, instead of focusing on every part of me that jiggles, my eyes are firmly locked on what his hands are doing to me.

I've never really watched much before, but holy shit, it's sexy as hell. His hands expertly give attention everywhere I crave it.

When I stare at my reflection, I don't feel repulsed or disgusted. The way Aiden's hands touch me and the way he's looking at me makes me feel beautiful—sexy even.

Leaning close to my ear, Aiden growls, "I need to taste

you."

Before I ask what he means, he spins me around and lifts me, so I'm sitting on the counter next to the sink. He kneels and settles between my thighs.

Using his thumb, he moves the material of my thong out of his way, giving his mouth easier access.

With a long swipe, he licks the length of my pussy. The sensation makes me shiver and cry out his name. Then, his tongue begins to devour me.

He props one of my legs up on the counter, completely spreading me for him. He wraps his fingers around my thigh, keeping me open for him.

That tongue of his is a gift from God as he laps against my clit.

When my thong keeps getting in his way—and preventing him from doing the lord's work—he gets frustrated. Grabbing it on either side, he rips it clean in half.

I don't know why seeing this caveman side of him turns me on so much, but damnit, it does.

Once there's nothing else in his way, Aiden dives back in, eating my pussy with such fervor my legs are shaking within moments. His tongue flicks across my clit, and I feel myself beginning to lose it.

When he slips two fingers inside my wet heat and finds that sweet spot, I start pulsing around him.

Noises that I've never heard myself make echo off the bathroom walls as my body quakes. As I come, he holds me even closer to his face, making sure he wrings every ounce of pleasure out of me.

When he stands back up, I whisper, "Wow. That was incredible."

"Oh, sweetheart, we aren't done yet," he says, pulling off his robe and yanking down his boxers.

His *thick-as-a-Coke-can* cock comes into view, and it's just as mesmerizing as it was last night. I'm not quite sure how it fit inside me. It seemed like magic, but I'm ready to see the party trick again.

"Shit," he growls. "I need to go get a condom."

He starts to leave the bathroom, but I lay my hand on his shoulder.

"You don't need it," I assure him. "I'm on the pill and haven't been with anyone since the last time I went to the doctor."

"Are you sure?" He asks, not wanting to push me into anything.

"Yes," I reply in barely more than a breathy whisper.

He walks back over to me and gives me a passionate, heated kiss before saying, "Fuck, woman. You're going to be the death of me."

He kisses me once more before turning me around. "Turn around, and set your hands on the counter," he instructs.

I do as he wishes, so I'm bent over the vanity, staring at myself in the mirror as Aiden positions himself behind me.

He lines himself up with my entrance and slips inside. I gasp, feeling his thickness stretch me as wide as I can go. There's no pain, though. It's all pleasure—mind-blowing pleasure.

"Watch us, baby. Watch me fuck you," he says in a low tone.

My eyes lock with his in the mirror, and I can see that his hold a fierce hunger. He slides in and out of me at a steady pace, drawing my eyes to where our two bodies are joined.

Every time he plunges into me, my ass juggles. Typically, I'd hate watching any part of me jiggle, but the way Aiden is staring at it tells me how much he's enjoying the view. It's further confirmed when his fingers grab the juicy flesh and push into me harder.

Every hard thrust is hitting all the right spots, bringing me closer to another orgasm. I moan his name, which spurs him on even more.

When he speeds up, I lose it. My body starts to collapse from the waves of pleasure crashing over me. He holds me up as he finds his release inside me.

When both of our bodies still, he leans forward and places a few soft kisses on my shoulder. He slides out of me and grabs a washcloth to clean us both up.

When he's finished, he gives me a slow, tender kiss. "Beautiful," he whispers as he pulls back.

As we make our way to the bed to lie down, my head is spinning with everything that has happened in just a couple of days.

My boss, who I've never thought of as more than a grumpy introvert, is actually sweet and funny—not to mention a fucking sex wizard.

*How could I have been so wrong about him?*

When we are situated under the blankets, I snuggle close to his warm body. He's like my own personal space heater.

"Do you want me to go back to my room?" He asks.

"Not a chance in hell," I reply. "You are so comfortable. You have to stay."

"Okay, sweetheart," he whispers before kissing the top of my head.

"Why are you so comfy?" I ask, slowly losing the battle with my heavy eyelids.

He chuckles. "It's my extra layer of meat. More comfortable than lying on some hard six-pack abs of all your frat boy exes?"

Half asleep, I reply, "Oh, Boss Man, they've got nothing on you."

# Chapter Fourteen

## AIDEN

The following morning, the smell of vanilla fills my nostrils. When I finally open my eyes, all I see is hair—a mess of long blonde hair.

As I lift my head, the strands of hair slip off my face, and I see that Romy is lying in the crook of my neck. She's facing away from me, but her body is still firmly pressed against mine.

Feeling her soft, curvy body completely naked next to me makes my dick begin to stir. But when I see what time it is, I tell my member that he will have to wait.

Pulling her close to me, I inhale deeply, sniffing the intoxicating aroma of her hair. She lets out a soft moan, and I once again have to tell my cock to play it cool.

I wrap my arm around her and start whispering in her ear. "Romy, sweetheart, it's time to wake up. Our classes start soon."

She just gives me a tired grunt.

I try again. "Come on, beautiful."

"I can't move. You've fucked me into a sex coma."

The corners of my lips curl into a smile. "I'm glad you liked it."

"Can't we just stay in bed all day?" She groans.

"How about we get up and get you some coffee? And then, later on, I'll try to replicate that sex coma."

Her eyes still closed, she grins. "Deal."

Slowly, she rolls out of bed and makes her way into the bathroom. I hear the shower come on, and I consider joining her, but then, we'd *never* get out of here.

Instead, I head to my own room to hop in the shower. I try not to take too long so that I can get back to Romy. She and I have a week together, and I intend to take full advantage of it and spend as much time with her as possible. Because for whatever reason, what we are doing feels inexplicably natural.

When I get back to Romy's room, she's still in the bathroom, but now she's doing her hair. She dollops a hefty amount of something called *Beachy Waves* into her palm and works it through from root to tip with her fingers.

The typical vanilla scent of her hair now mingles with the coconut smell of the product.

She's wearing nothing more than a bra and thong, and I'm glad to see she's feeling a little more comfortable in her skin. If nothing else, by the end of the week, I want Romy to have some idea of exactly how gorgeous she is.

She sees me staring, and I try to play it off. Leaning down, I pick up the scraps of her torn thong, which was still on the bathroom floor.

"Sorry I ripped your panties," I say, holding up the two pieces.

Her shoulders shrug. "It's okay. These damn thongs drive me crazy anyway."

"Why?" I ask.

She turns toward me and gestures toward the panties she's wearing. "Look at them. They fit me fine, yet half my vagina hangs out. It's like if you're not thin, it gets harder to find sexy underwear that fit as they should." Her arms fly through the air as she speaks, showing her annoyance on the matter.

"Okay, next question," I say. "Why wear them?"

She turns back to face the mirror and messes with her hair again. "The underwear was another one of Veronica's bright ideas. I wouldn't have packed these. These were my 'skinny' panties."

I take a step toward her. "No, Romy, you misunderstand me. I mean, why wear panties at all? I'd have much easier access if you didn't."

That gets her attention, making her stop and stare at me.

"Boss Man, if you keep saying things like that and putting dirty thoughts in my head, you'll miss your classes." Her finger pokes into my chest. "And I need some coffee."

I'd be lying if I said I'm not thinking about having a replay of last night, right here and now, but I push the thought from my mind. Instead, I give Romy a smile and wink and walk out of the bathroom.

I let Romy finish getting ready while I run downstairs to get us some coffee.

Thankfully, the line isn't long, and when I get back, Romy is all ready to head out.

Today, she's wearing a floral tank top with a pretty necklace attached to it and a pair of black jeans. She looks beautiful—as usual.

"What's on the agenda today?" I ask.

Although I already know which seminar I'm attending this morning, I know Romy has an entire schedule all written up. And sure enough, she walks over to the table and grabs a folder off of it. She opens it and pulls out a neatly typed itinerary.

Her eyes glance over the sheet. "You are going to *How to Maximize your Staff*, and I'm going to *How to Acquire Repeat Customers.*

"Both of them sound thrilling," I tease.

"No joke. After that, there's some sort of team-building mixer thing."

"That's even worse."

She giggles. "Agreed. But we are here. We might as well learn everything we can."

We leave the room and head downstairs, coffees in hand.

When we part ways downstairs, I stare at Romy's ass as she walks away. Thoughts of that ass bouncing as I bent her over last night flash through my mind.

I struggle to push them out, ready to try to concentrate on whatever this speaker has to say.

But everything reminds me of Romy. And it's not all sexual. Some of it is thinking back to something funny she said or the way her nose crinkles when she laughs.

It's time to accept a fundamental fact—Romy Sinclair has set up shop in my head, and it doesn't look like she's going anywhere any time soon.

Even after our week is over.

# Chapter Fifteen

## ROMY

My knee frantically bobs up and down as I impatiently wait for this seminar to end. I've barely paid attention at all. I know I should, but I can't help it. The topic is yet again something that I'm already well-educated in.

I mean, my inability to focus *obviously doesn't* have anything to do with Aiden Montgomery or his magic tongue.

Or his expert cock.

Or his striking good looks.

Okay, all of that is a lie. I'm thinking about all of those things—not to mention how sweet he is and how good he makes me feel about myself.

Yes, Aiden is certainly turning out to be everything I never imagined him to be.

I wonder if he's sitting in his seminar thinking about me. Oh my goodness, listen to me. I sound like a high school girl whose crush is in a different class down the hall.

Fuck it. I don't care.

I consider pulling out my phone and sending him a dirty text to ensure that he's thinking about me, but maybe I'm not quite adventurous enough for that.

Not yet anyway.

Instead, I stay trapped in my thoughts until the speaker finally wraps things up. When he does, I walk out into the hallway and see the team-building mixer is starting in the big ball-room across the hall.

The doors to the room Aiden is in are still closed, so I fire off a text telling him to meet me in the mixer. My throat is dry, and hopefully, this thing has some refreshments.

My eyes scan the large room as I walk in and immediately zero in on the food table. I head straight for it and grab one of the bottles of water sitting on the end.

Opening it, I chug half of it down and look for a corner to hide in until Aiden gets here. He's the only person I even re-motely want to interact with.

But when a random guy comes walking up to talk to me, I realize I'm not going to get that lucky. He's not a bad-looking guy —reminds me of a Ken doll. But he's no Aiden.

Not even close.

"You look a little out of place," he says, showing off teeth that are so perfect I'm convinced they're veneers.

"Should I be offended?" I ask.

"Not at all. I was just thinking how someone as gorgeous as you stands out in a room full of testosterone."

"Maybe it's just a lack of options." I put forth my strongest sarcasm, but he doesn't pick up on it.

"No, I don't think that's it." He looks at me with lust-filled eyes, but not in the same way Aiden does. This guy is creepy with the way he's leering at me.

When I don't say anything, he adds, "What are you doing here all alone, honey?"

Before I can even open my mouth to respond, a deep voice comes from behind me, filling the silence.

"She's not alone."

*Aiden.*

He stands beside me, and I feel his fingers lightly graze my arm. I know I said we should keep a low profile while in public, but I don't think I've ever been happier to see him, and I want this other guy to get the hint and go away.

So, I wrap my arms around his waist and lean up to kiss

him. It's just a short peck on the lips, but it's enough to get the Ken doll to walk away.

Once he's gone, I look up at Aiden. "Sorry. I know I said no PDA, but I needed to get rid of that guy."

He smiles. "Oh, I'm not complaining. I'll never give up a chance to have you in my arms. Besides, I would have done it if you hadn't just to get rid of him. But are you starting to believe me when I say you're beautiful?"

I shake my head. "As I told him, it's a lack of options. I'm one of the only women here."

"No, you're stunning." He turns me around, so I'm facing the sea of people that's filing in. He wraps his arms around my stomach and leans in to whisper, "Do you know how many men in this room would love to take you to bed?"

"Uhm...one."

"No, sweetheart. That's how many *are* going to take you to bed tonight."

I swallow the lump in my throat at the mere thought of him taking me to bed.

"We have to wait until tonight?" I ask with a slight pout.

I feel his body shake with laughter. "I guess we don't have to, but I had something else in mind if you're interested."

"I'm listening."

"Well, I was thinking you and I could head down to the beach for a while."

"The beach?"

He nods. "It should be pretty dead since everyone seems to be in here. We can grab a couple of drinks and relax for the afternoon.

I smile from ear to ear. "Sounds perfect."

We leave the room as discreetly as we can and make our way back upstairs. Each of us heads to our own room to change clothes. I'm tempted just to tell Aiden to move his suitcase over here since the only time he ever leaves me is to change clothes or shower.

Maybe we can just shower together—to conserve water, of

course. That's the *only* reason I'm even thinking about it.

I chuckle at how even in my head, I don't believe myself.

The moment I unzip my suitcase, dread washes over me. I completely forgot about the fact that Veronica switched out my swimsuit. The item that replaces my modest tankini is a tiny hot pink bikini.

"Fuck you, Veronica," I mutter.

I consider telling Aiden I changed my mind about going to the beach. I'm sure that I could convince him that staying in bed all day is a better idea.

But I *do* want to swim in the ocean. Who knows the next time I'll be in a tropical paradise? I don't want to wait another thirty years for this opportunity.

Upon further inspection, I see that Veronica did leave my cover-up in here, so at least I'll have a little bit of a shield. And hopefully, Aiden's right, and there aren't a ton of people down there.

Without wasting any more time, I change into the bikini and put the cover-up on over it. I walk into the bathroom and throw my hair into a high ponytail. I put some drops in my eyes to help deal with my annoying contact lenses and then use my razor to shave a couple of patches on my thighs, which I missed in the shower this morning.

Soon after I finish, Aiden is knocking on the door.

When I pull it open, I see he's wearing a pair of red swim trunks and a gray ribbed tank top.

It's so weird seeing Aiden Montgomery, a man who thrives in the cold, in beachwear. But I'm not complaining.

He looks sexy as hell.

"Hey, are you ready?" He asks with a smile.

"Yep," I say, grabbing my room key and asking him to hold onto it for me.

When the door closes behind me, we make our way down the hallway, and I say, "You know you don't have to knock on the front door? Our rooms are adjoining."

"I told you I wouldn't use it without your permission."

*Such a gentleman.*

"Aiden, we're sleeping together. You have made me come with just your tongue...twice. I think you have permission to use our shared door."

His mouth curls up into a half-smile. "Noted."

"So, when was the last time you went to the beach?" I ask as we step onto the elevator.

"Oh man," he says, rubbing his beard and trying to remember. "At least twenty years. Allison and I were kids when our parents took us, and I'm pretty sure we only went the one time."

"Didn't care for the beach, huh?"

"We had a good time, but typically, we would go to the mountains on our vacations."

"Of course, you did," I laugh. "Is your whole family cold-blooded like you?"

"Pretty much," he says, smiling down at me.

"Did you guys go on vacation a lot?" I ask.

He nods. "Every year. They were never anything fancy, but my parents made sure we had that time together every single year."

I think back to my own childhood. My parents had more money than they knew what to do with, but we never took family vacations. I'm sure it had something to do with the fact that my father was breaking a ton of laws to acquire his fortune, and my mother was fucking the pool boy.

As the elevator doors open, Aiden grabs my hand as we step off. Thinking about my fucked up family slightly changed my demeanor, and I think he noticed.

He doesn't let my hand go the entire time it takes to get to the beach.

The moment we step out the back doors of the resort onto the path, the warm air blowing off the waves whips around me. The salty smell fills my lungs as I inhale deeply.

When we get to the sand, both of us bend over to take off our sandals. Sand between our toes, we walk closer to the water.

A beach attendant walks over to greet us and then leads us

to a row of empty lounge chairs. Aiden was right—there's no one else out here besides a couple of stragglers walking up and down near the surf.

The attendant asks if we would like anything from the bar.

Aiden looks at me, waiting for my answer.

"Something tall, fruity, and frozen," I say with a smile. "Surprise me."

Aiden turns back toward the attendant. "Two tall, fruity frozen drinks, please."

The man walks off, and each of us takes a seat in a lounger. I gaze out over the water, and I'm amazed at the vastness of it. People always talk about how breathtaking the ocean is, but you can never really take in the full gravity of it until you're here, right in front of it.

"What do you think, beautiful?" Aiden asks me.

"It's…it's…amazing." I don't know how else to describe it.

"Yes, it is," he agrees.

The never-ending cascading waves mesmerize me. I'm almost hypnotized watching them crash against the shore.

I'm so enthralled that I barely hear the attendant return with our cocktails. Aiden takes both large cups and hands one to me before giving the man a hefty tip.

I sip the fruity concoction, and it's delicious—some sort of strawberry pineapple thing with rum in it.

So good.

I take a few long sips but decide that in this heat, I better slow down.

We both lean back in our chairs, letting the sun warm us as we sit in comfortable silence. I'm convinced this is indeed the meaning of the word 'paradise.' Minnesota and its shitty weather are an entire world away.

I have no idea how long we lie there, but after a while, the sun starts to warm me—maybe a little too much. It's beginning to beat down on my skin, and this cover-up isn't helping to keep me cool.

"Do you want to get in the water?" I ask Aiden.

"Yeah, let's go." He stands up and starts to head toward the big blue ocean.

"Are you going to take your shirt off?" I ask.

He smiles. "Only if you take yours off." He looks at my cover-up.

He pulls the tank top over his head, exposing his chest and stomach. I could stare at him all day.

But as he pulls his hair back into a low ponytail, he says, "Your turn."

I glance around to make sure no one is staring before I slip off the light material. I try to suck in my gut, but there's only so far it will go. Plus, I can't breathe, so I let out the breath I was holding and hold toward the water.

Aiden is already wading up to his waist. I let out a slight squeal as the cold water flows over my toes.

He whips around to make sure I'm okay. When he sees my swimsuit, his eyes go wide.

Blushing, I say, "Another one of Veronica's bright ideas."

"Okay, forget a thank-you card. Remind me to send that woman a whole damn gift basket."

# Chapter Sixteen

## AIDEN

*H*oly fuck! What is she wearing?!
Romy took off that over-shirt thing and sur-prised me with the tiny bikini underneath. Let's just say I'm happy that I'm in water deep enough to cover my bottom half.

As she walks toward me, she keeps stopping to let herself adjust to the water. The cool temperature is making her nipples protrude through the thin material of her top.

I want them in my mouth right fucking now.

"What?" She asks when she sees me gawking.

"You look...perfect."

"Ha!" She yells. "You're so full of shit. I'm sure I look like a cow in this thing."

"No," I sternly reply. "You look amazing. And if you dis-agree, I'll just have to prove it to you when I peel that bikini off your body."

"Oh, I'm going to keep arguing because I *definitely* want that to happen," she says with a smirk.

Lord, I want to bend her over my knee and spank that juicy ass of hers.

She's been standing in the same spot for a while now, so I ask, "You coming?"

"In a minute. It's chilly."

"You'll never get used to it if you don't take the plunge."

Her eyes grow wide as I walk toward her. "Aiden, what are you doing?"

I step through the water with sheer determination until I reach her and then lift her into my arms. With one arm around her shoulders and the other under her knees, I head back out into the waves.

"Aiden!" She squeals through her giggles.

Her arms lock around my neck, and her face buries in my chest as she braces for the next wave to hit us.

She's squeezing her eyes shut while still laughing her head off.

Walking further into the water, I say, "You better brace yourself, baby."

The water collects into a giant wave — bigger than I thought it would be. I hold onto her tight and close my eyes as the water crashes over our heads.

When the wave subsides, I expect her to yell at me for getting her drenched. But she doesn't.

Instead, she just wipes the water from her eyes and lets out another giggle.

"I think I'm used to it now," she says.

I set her back down on her feet, and she takes my hand. We walk a little further out into the surf, and we have a ton of fun jumping up and trying to ride the waves.

A huge swell hits us, and it takes us both under. When we come up for air, immediately my eyes are drawn to her chest, where one of her nipples has popped free of her top.

She notices my eyes, which are now bulging out of my head, and looks down.

"Oh, shit!" She gasps and struggles to fix the garment.

When her boobs are contained once again, she looks down and back at me. "Is that better?"

I give her a sly smile. "I liked it better the other way."

"I bet you did, but that doesn't mean everyone else on the beach needs a show."

My eyes scan up and down the shore, and sure as hell, there's not another soul around. "Who are you worried about?" I ask.

Her eyes look where mine just did. "Oh. Well, still."

Grabbing her by the hand, I pull her toward me until our bodies press together. I can feel her hard nipples pressing into my chest.

When one of my hands runs along her side, I use my thumb to lightly graze the stiff peak.

She sighs, and her big eyes flick up at me. "You're a filthy boss. Do you know that?"

"You should take it up with HR," I whisper.

"Oh yeah? And who would that be?"

I smile. "Also me."

A smile spreads across her lips. "Oh, well then, I would like to tell HR that I have a filthy boss."

I nod. "Would you like to file a formal complaint?"

"No, actually, I think I need some therapy because I'm pretty obsessed with how dirty he is."

Before she can utter another word, I lift her out of the water and wrap her legs around me. I use one hand to hold her under her ass and the other to tangle in her hair while I kiss her.

Her arms link around my neck, pulling me deeper into our kiss. I love her enthusiasm as we stand there making out. She acts like my kiss is the oxygen she needs to breathe.

I turn us so we face the vast blue sea, shielding us from prying eyes that might happen to walk by.

Once I'm comfortable that we are out of eyesight, I tell her to hold on tight so that I can have some fun. She tightens her grip around my neck and firmly locks her legs around my waist.

With my hands free, I pull each side of her top off to the side, exposing her large tits. Her nipples harden even more when they're free.

My fingers start to play and tease, driving Romy wild in the process. She throws her head back and moans my name, driving me just as crazy.

My cock swells and tests the material of my swim trunks. Romy takes notice and moves her hips, rubbing against the tip.

"And you think *I'm* dirty? If you're not careful, I'm going to fuck you right here in the ocean."

Her tongue runs across her bottom lip. "How about we go upstairs and do that instead?" She reaches underneath her and gives my dick a firm squeeze through my shorts.

"Oh, sweetheart, the things I'm going to do to you and that sexy body of yours," I growl.

She peels herself off of me and sets her feet back down in the sand before pulling her top back into place to contain her tits again—just barely.

We start to make our way back to the shore, but I stop before the water gets any more shallow than my waist.

Turning around, Romy asks, "What's wrong? What are you doing?"

Clearing my throat, I say, "I need to stay here for a minute —until my *problem* goes away." My eyes dart down to my still-hard cock.

"Ah," she smiles. "You don't want anyone to see your Coke can?"

My eyebrows shoot up. "Coke can?"

"That's what I'm calling that beast living in your pants. It's about the same size—and you know, it's complete with that high-fructose *porn* syrup."

That makes me laugh so hard I can barely breathe. "That's a new one. Should I be offended?"

"Uhm, no. Have you seen how thick a Coke can is? I'm honestly surprised it fits."

"Oh, sweetheart, I know how to get you wet enough to make it fit."

She points her finger at me. "Hey, stop that. You're not going to make *it* any less excited talking like that."

*True.*

She continues, "Besides, I think you should just get out of the water anyway. I mean, you whipped out my titties for the whole world to see."

"There was no one around. You know I wouldn't have let anyone else see those works of art."

Her head turns back and forth, glancing all around. "I don't see anyone else around right now."

"Oh, yeah?"

She nods before using her fingers to pull the material off of her nipples once more. She squeezes her large breasts together before pinching the hard buds.

"Romy," I warn. "You're making my dick even harder."

"Oh, really? What are you going to do about it, Mr. Montgomery?"

A switch flips in my head, and I can't take anymore. Hard-on or not, I move toward Romy and scoop her up, tossing her over my shoulder.

Her chest is pressed against me, ensuring no one can see her goods. I carry her through the water and continue onto the beach.

She giggles as she bounces up and down with every step I take. "You can put me down."

"Are your tits still hanging out?" I ask.

"...maybe."

"Then, no, I can't." I take one of my hands and smack her ass before grabbing a handful.

Just as I turn a corner to head back inside the resort, I stop just short of running smack dab into two people.

But not just any two people—the elderly couple from the elevator.

Their eyes go wide at the sight of me carrying Romy like a caveman while smacking her ass.

"What's wrong?" Romy asks. "Why'd we stop? I thought you were anxious to get all up in my lady bits. I need your Coke-can penis. If I shake it up and down really hard, will it explode?"

That makes them even more mortified, but Romy can't stop giggling at her own joke.

"Nice to see you again," I say, walking past them.

"Who are you talking to?" Romy asks. When she lifts her head and sees them walking away, she laughs even harder. "Oh, shit!"

I don't set her back on her feet until we are safely in the elevator. She adjusts her top, pushing everything back into place.

"I forgot my cover-up on the beach," she gasps.

"We'll get it later," I assure.

"Do you think it will still be there?"

"If not, I'll buy you a new one," I promise. "Trust me, tonight, I don't want a single inch of you covered up."

Once the doors open, I grab her hand, and we hurry to her room. I pull her key out of my pocket and unlock the door.

When we're inside, I immediately push her against the wall and kiss her while pinning her arms above her head.

From her vanilla scent to her sweet taste to the way her curvy body makes my dick impossibly hard, Romy is intoxicating. Every part of her has a hold on me.

When my lips release hers, I rub my thumb across her swollen bottom lip. "Let's go take a shower."

She nods as her tongue darts out and licks my thumb.

*Dear lord, she's going to kill me.*

Grabbing her hand once more, I lead her into the bathroom. I reach in to turn on the hot water and give it time to warm up.

While we wait, I take my time untying the small bows holding her swimsuit together around her body. When each of the strings is undone, it slips off her body and onto the floor.

Then, her fingers make quick work of untying my trunks and pulling them down my legs. My dick had calmed down until she gives it a few slow strokes, and my boner returns with a vengeance.

As to not blow my load all over her hand, I lead us both into the large walk-in shower. The warm water washes over both of us as I kiss her again. My tongue takes its time exploring her mouth while my hands roam over her skin.

Although it starts slow and sensual, it doesn't take long to become frenzied and hungry.

She pulls back from our kiss with a wild look in her eyes. Before I can ask what she's thinking, she sinks to her knees, getting settled on the floor of the shower.

I can't imagine it's very comfortable, but before I can tell her she doesn't have to, her tongue flicks out and swirls around the head of my cock.

It feels so good that it takes every ounce of me not to let my legs turn to jelly. And when she widens her jaw and takes me as deep as she can, oh my lord.

It's fucking incredible.

With one hand, I brace myself against the shower wall while the other holds onto her ponytail. I wrap the hair around my knuckles but still let her set the pace.

The way Romy alternates between deep, slow sucks and quick, light licks makes every nerve in my body come to life. The woman sucks my cock like it's the best fucking popsicle she's ever had.

"Fuck, Romy," I groan.

She gives a sexy moan in response, making her mouth vibrate against me while she sucks.

As much as I'd love to fill her mouth with my release, I pull her back to her feet because I'm nowhere near done with her. I turn her around and tell her to brace herself against the wall. But when I try to slide inside her heat, it's just awkward. Our height differences and the fact we are all wet make it hard to get any traction or momentum going.

I turn her toward me once more and try to hold up one of her legs and do it that way, but it's not working either.

Romy's eyes glance around. "Where's the bench? Don't these things usually have benches?"

I chuckle. "Why does shower sex always sound better in theory than it turns out to actually be?"

"I have no idea, but we have a nice big bed out there we can continue this on."

Without even responding, I shut off the valve, and the water abruptly stops. I grab each of us a towel, and we quickly dry off.

Romy exits the bathroom first, and I finish drying off. When I make my way back to the bedroom, Romy is lying on the bed, completely naked and waiting for me.

When she notices me, her knees fall open, giving me a glimpse of her pretty pussy.

As perfect as this moment is, there's one thought that I just can't seem to shake.

*How the hell am I going to give this up after our week is over?*

# Chapter Seventeen

## ROMY

"Holy shit!" I cry out as Aiden gives me my third orgasm and finds his own.

My body tenses so hard that I get a pain in my thigh leading all the way up my butt cheek.

"Cramp!" I squeal, writhing around in pain.

Aiden uses his large hands to massage it until the pain subsides.

When we're lying next to each other once again, I say, "Damn, I feel like I need another shower. I think our last one made us even dirtier."

He smiles and wipes the sweat from his brow. "Well, we can try, but you're going to have to keep your hands to yourself."

"Oh, don't start with me, Boss Man," I tease. "Let's go."

We walk back into the bathroom, but this time, our shower isn't nearly as eventful. We wash our bodies and get the salt out of our hair. It's not overly sexy or romantic, as both of us are just in a hurry to get it done.

Once we finish, we lie back in bed, but it's too early to go to sleep, and neither one of us want to get dressed to go anywhere.

'Room service it is!" I announce.

Instead of cheeseburgers again, this time, we get some pizzas and beer.

While we wait for the food, I walk around the room looking for something to do. Finally, I pull open a drawer in an end table and spot a deck of cards.

"Want to play?" I ask, holding it up.

"Sure. What's the game?"

"Poker or Go Fish. Take your pick."

His face scrunches up. "Uh, duh. Go Fish."

A smile spreads across my lips as we sit down across the table from each other. I deal us out some cards and set the rest in a neat stack between us.

When I pick up my cards, immediately, I have three pairs, which I match and set off to the side.

"Cheater," he mumbles, not having any pairs of his own to lay down.

"Do you want to play Twenty Questions while we play this?" I ask.

His brow furrows. "Twenty Questions where we try to guess which item the other person is thinking?"

My head shakes back and forth. "No. More like we get to know each other better Think of it like Truth or Dare—without the Dare."

"But the Dare is the best part," he says with a playful wink.

"How about later on you can dare me to do whatever you want?" I challenge.

He stares at his cards and shakes his head. "Sweetheart, you have to stop saying things like that, or we're never going to get to play any sort of games—except the naked kind."

I can't help but smile. "Down, boy. You'll get your chance later on."

"Hey, I can be patient. The one-eyed weasel, though? That's a different story."

"Yeah, yeah. Do you have any twos?"

He glances down. "Go fish. Okay, beautiful, ask for your first question."

I think for a moment, trying to pick out the perfect one. While picking up a card from the deck, I blurt, "How many women have you slept with?"

*That's my perfect question?!*

Aiden's eyes briefly glance up at me before looking back at his cards. "Do you have any aces?"

I take the ace of diamonds out of my hand and give it to him.

Pausing, I don't ask for another card just yet. Instead, I wait for him to answer my question.

He takes a deep breath and lets it out as a sigh before beginning to speak. "Five. I've slept with five women."

My eyebrows raise so high they practically touch my hairline. "Only five?"

"Is that a bad thing?"

"No, not at all," I stammer. "Just surprising is all. You are way too good at sex to have only been with five women."

"Well, thank you. But just because it was only five women doesn't mean I didn't get in my fair share of practice with those five women."

Oh, I can certainly believe that. If Aiden Montgomery were my man, I'd be taking a ride on that pogo stick every chance I got. But I have to say that my number is more than double that which makes me feel a little slutty.

*What can I say? College was a crazy time for me.*

And the fact that his number is lower than mine, and he's still better at sex than me, means I'm not even good at being slutty.

In an attempt to get out of my head, I clear my throat and ask, "Do you have any seven's?"

He takes a card and hands it to me. "And my question to you is: do you have any siblings?"

"You're not going to ask about my number?"

He shakes his head. "I don't need to know. It might prompt thoughts of you fucking other guys, and I'd rather just imagine you fucking me."

"Makes sense. And to answer your question, no, I don't have any siblings."

He asks me for another card, and I tell him to go fish. "So,

83

why only five?" I don't know why I just can't let this go.

His eyes narrow as he stares at his cards. "I don't know. I mean, I never had the traditional college experience of dating around and all that. Usually, I was too exhausted to be out chasing tail, and I guess I've always just been more of a one-woman kind of guy. I try to do everything I can to keep that one woman happy, but I'm still not great at that, though."

I seriously doubt that. Aiden and I aren't even actually dating, and he's treated me better than any man I've ever been with.

We keep playing the game while continuing to ask each other questions.

When it's his turn again, he says, "Tell me about your parents."

"What do you want to know?" I shift uncomfortably in my seat. "That's a bit of a loaded question."

"Whatever you're comfortable telling me."

Oh boy, that's a touchy subject. So, I take a moment to collect my thoughts and figure out what I want to share.

*Fuck it. I'm just going to lay it all out.*

"My parents were…distant. Their idea of affection was handing me a credit card and telling me to buy myself something pretty. I was raised by nannies when I was young, and when I hit puberty, they left me to fend for myself."

"Shit, Romy. That's rough," Aiden says.

I can feel his eyes on me, but I avoid his gaze. "It is what it is. I never knew any different."

"It still doesn't make it right."

"No, it doesn't," I mutter, almost too quietly to hear.

"So, I have to ask—if your parents are well-off, what are you doing working for me?" He gives a slight smile as he asks.

"Oh, I was just drawn to your overall sunny disposition." I return his grin. "Besides, I said my parents *were* well-off—not that they still are."

"Does that have anything to do with what you said happened in college that turned your life around?"

I pause once more before responding. I've never told this

story to anyone besides Veronica. Even the people I hung out with at the time thought I just became a prude because I never told them anything else.

But something about Aiden makes me want to confide in him—to tell him personal things I don't usually share. I'm still unsure as to whether or not that is a good thing.

We exchange a couple more cards and set down more pairs before I answer.

"When I was in college, my father was arrested for fraud. It turns out all of the money he'd made had come from some very elaborate pyramid schemes. The feds raided my parents' house and seized everything."

"Damn," Aiden says. "I take it there was no money left for your college?"

"Something like that. After shit hit the fan and my father got arrested, my mother claimed she knew nothing, and the cops couldn't prove otherwise, so she was cleared of any wrongdoing. She filed for divorce and had a new rich husband before the ink on the papers even dried—although she's probably still fucking whatever pool boy she has. That was always her signature move.

"After my dad was locked up, I refused to go see him, so he started writing me letters. In them, he told me he had some off-shore bank accounts I could take money out of. He gave me the account and routing numbers and told me the money was all mine since he'd probably be locked up for the rest of his life. I only ever wrote him one letter in return. I told him I didn't want his money, and I'd never touch the accounts. It would always just be a reminder of how he loved money more than he loved me. So, I stopped partying and buckled down. I took out some student loans and have worked my butt off to pay them back."

We are both quiet for a moment. When we finally break the silence, Aiden is the first one to speak. "Wow, Romy, I—"

But I stop him. "Aiden, I didn't tell you any of this for pity. That's the absolute last thing I want."

He sets his cards down in front of him before speaking

again. "Oh Romy, I know damn well you don't need my pity. And I *don't* pity you. On the contrary, I have a crazy amount of respect for anyone who can turn their life around and come out on the other side stronger than before. that takes big brass ones, baby."

I can't help but smile a little. It's crazy how this man can still make me smile even while I discuss the most fucked up event in my life.

But I'm beyond ready to change the subject and get this glaring spotlight off of myself.

"Okay, Boss Man, I believe you asked like six questions in a row."

He runs his fingers through his dark hair, pushing it out of his face. "Sorry, you're just too intriguing for your own good."

"Uh-huh, sure. But since it's my turn, why don't you tell me what happened with Jane?"

As if the universe steps in, there's a knock on the door before he can answer me. He stands up to grab our pizza and beer.

I move all of our cards aside to make room to set the pizza on the table before grabbing us each a paper plate. Once he's back, I put a slice on each of the plates and hand one over.

As I take the first bite, I mutter, "Well, it's better than the cheeseburgers last night, but I could name at least five pizza places back home who put this to shame."

"Are you some sort of pizza guru?" He asks, taking a big bite out of his slice.

"Oh, yeah. Remember that thing about how I don't cook? Most of the pizza delivery drivers know me by name."

He laughs. "Hey, I get it. I love a good pizza too."

I open my mouth to tell him that I could show him the best pizza joints in town when we return to Minnesota, but I immediately snap it back closed.

Because this whole thing is temporary. That's what I wanted and what we agreed to, right? There's going to be none of this when we go back home. After a week, it all ends.

Sadness washes over me, but I try to push it from my mind. I don't want to ruin the rest of our week.

I take a deep breath and try to change the subject. "Hey, Boss Man, don't think you're going to get out of answering my question. I told you my sob story. Time to tell me about Jane."

"Damn, I thought you'd forgotten," he teases with a wink.

"You know me better than that."

He takes another bite and swallows it down before answering.

"Jane and I met when I was just starting the business. We met at a birthday party for a mutual friend. She was sweet, and we had a lot of fun. I would work during the day, and she'd plan our evenings. Over time, we were practically living together. Jane didn't work, but I didn't mind. She handled the housework and the cooking—all the stuff I didn't want to do. We each did our fair share.

"But as time went on, I got busier with trying to get the business up and running. I wasn't home a lot during the evenings, and when I was, I was typically too tired to do anything. I tried to give her attention still and make sure she felt appreciated, but I just couldn't do it all. She hated that I worked so much and would go shopping and spend money while I worked, which made me feel like I needed to work more to get the business up and running."

He pauses for a moment before continuing. "I suggested she try to find a hobby—something that brought her joy. She started taking yoga classes, and then that slowly transformed into a whole healthy kick. She became obsessed with losing weight. I thought she was great before, but if she wanted to do something that made her feel better about herself, I wasn't going to stop her. She started spending all her time at the gym and eventually came to me and confessed she'd been sleeping with her trainer and was leaving me to go be with him."

"What a bitch," I say, reaching for another slice of pizza.

Aiden crosses his arms over his chest. "Eh, I don't know. She made some good points. I probably should have appreciated her more and made her more of a priority."

I stop him. "No, fuck that! Aiden, first of all, I can't imagine that you completely ignored this woman. I bet you were still wonderful to her, and even if you didn't, that's no excuse for an affair. If she was that unhappy, she should've just left."

"And second of all, so what if you didn't dote on her twenty-four hours a day? Part of a relationship is being there for the other person when they need you. It's giving 75% when the other person only has 25% in the tank. You don't give up on someone when they're chasing their dreams."

I realize I've gone off on a rant and try to dial it back a bit. "I just mean you seem like a good guy—you *are* a good guy. That shouldn't be taken for granted."

I've avoided looking at him this whole time, and when I finally do make eye contact, he's giving me a warm smile.

"Thanks, Romy. It's always nice to hear that," he replies.

I feel like we've stepped into a bit of an awkward situation, so I opt to change the subject once again.

"Are you ready for a card game a little more challenging?" I ask.

"Poker?"

"Yep. Do you play?"

He smiles. "It's been a while, but I think I remember."

I collect all the cards and shuffle them before handing them to Aiden to deal.

We decide on Five Card Draw. Before Aiden can start passing out the cards, I stop him.

"We don't have any chips to play with," I say, looking around, trying to find something that will work.

"We could always play Strip Poker," he offers.

I look down at what I'm wearing. "We both are wearing just our robes. It'd be a pretty quick game."

He shrugs. "I'm okay with that. I don't want to wait that long to get you naked anyway."

I feel my cheeks blush. "Oh yeah?"

"Yep. But here's a better idea—a little wager."

"Oh, I can't wait to hear this."

He leans on the table, his elbows resting on the cool wood.

"Whoever wins gets…special kisses…from the other."

"Special kisses?"

He opens his mouth to explain, but the lightbulb in my head flicks on, and I exclaim, *"Ohhhh, special kisses!* You mean like?" I point to my open mouth.

He chuckles and rubs his beard. "Yes. If you win, I spend the next hour with my face buried in your pussy. If I win, you give me a blow job."

Hearing Aiden talk dirty gives me the same reaction every time—it has me panting like a damn dog.

"Deal," I say.

"Okay, then," he grins.

"No, I mean deal. Deal the cards. Let's see who's going to get a happy ending tonight."

He begins to pass out the cards, but he looks up at me while he does it. "No matter who wins, I fully intend to make sure we both have our happy endings."

I pick up my five cards and take a look at them. Two 8's and two jacks. Two pairs—not bad.

When he asks how many cards I want, I say only one. He hands me a new card, and he taps his finger on the table, trying to figure out how many he wants. He finally settles on four.

*Four? How bad is his hand?*

When I look at my new card, I see it's another jack—Full House—jacks over 8's.

*I've got him now.*

I wait patiently for Aiden to analyze his new cards. After he's finished, he looks up at me again.

"Okay, Romy. Show me what you've got."

Laying down my cards, I taunt, "Read 'em and weep, Boss Man."

He looks at my hand and smiles. "You win."

I cheer and jump up and down. Would I be this excited to win if the prize wasn't a delicious Aiden-induced orgasm?

Probably not.

But that *is* my prize, and I'm going to love every second of it.

"Go lie down. I'll be right there," he says before excusing himself to the restroom.

Just for shits and giggles, I take a peek at his hand, which is now lying face down on the table. My eyes go wide when I see what he was holding.

A Royal Flush.

The best hand you can have in Poker.

And he lied and said he'd lost just to make me happy.

*Have I mentioned how perfect he is?*

# Chapter Eighteen

## AIDEN

"You know, eventually, we are going to have to go to some more of those seminars?" Romy asks me as we lounge on the beach.

"I know. But not today."

"I just feel bad that you brought me here, and because of me, you're missing out on a wealth of knowledge." She talks with her hands for emphasis. "I'm a bad influence on you."

"Romy, it was *my* idea to play hooky today—not yours."

She interrupts, "Because you felt like it's what *I* wanted."

She's cute when she gets all flustered.

"Romy, calm down. There weren't any classes that interested me today. It's alright, I promise."

"Okay," she snaps her mouth shut but immediately opens it again. "I'm just saying that I feel bad that you spent a ton of money to bring us here, and I don't want it to go to waste."

"Exactly. I spent the money, so I get to choose what I do or don't want to go to. Now, will you please drop it? We are supposed to be relaxing."

She leans back in her chair, adjusting the bun on top of her head. "You're right," she agrees.

We're quiet for a little while before she says, "It's beautiful out here, isn't it?"

"It sure is." When I say the words, my eyes aren't staring at the beach or the ocean. My gaze is fixed firmly on Romy.

I find myself staring at her constantly. She's fucking gorgeous, and I just can't seem to get enough.

Last night, when we were talking about Jane, she surprised me. Although Jane cheated on me, I still feel like I mostly come off as the bad guy. People assume that she had a legitimate reason to cheat because I wasn't giving her what she needed.

I've been guilty of thinking that myself plenty of times. I've beat myself up for years.

But when I told Romy, she stood in my corner and backed me up.

I guess she's always been backing me up in her own unique way. As I said before, my business wouldn't be what it is today if it weren't for Romy being in my corner and keeping me on track.

I remember when I first hired Romy. She spent her first month following every command I gave her—never questioning me. When she came to me asking if we could have a meeting, I was surprised. I was even more so when she came prepared with a presentation on how to streamline some of our systems.

The mousy girl I'd hired the month before was replaced with a woman who had a head full of ideas and was beyond excited to share them with me. After that day, I let her take over most of the day-to-day tasks around the office. She seemed to like having more responsibility, and I liked not handling any of the bullshit.

She truly has no idea how much easier she makes my life.

I still call her my assistant, but the truth is that she's been much more than that for years. I wonder if maybe it's time to step up and give her a better job title—something more fitting for how much she truly brings to the table.

And when she told me about everything she went through with her parents, it made me even more in awe of all that she does.

I'm not too proud to admit that I wouldn't be where I am today without my incredibly supportive parents. I couldn't have come as far as s I have without them.

Although Romy didn't start her own business, she's built a new life without anyone's help. That takes some big brass ones.

My eyes glance over at her. She's leaned back in the blue lounge chair, eyes closed as the sun beats down on her. Her hair is pulled into a loose bun on top of her head, but a few wild strands blow around in the breeze.

My gaze can't help but move down to drink in her curves, which are on full display thanks to her tiny swimsuit.

The pink fabric barely does enough to contain her ample breasts, and I feel my cock stirring to life as it yearns to slide between the two peaks while she stares up at me with those beautiful eyes.

I need to stop thinking dirty thoughts before I'm sporting a full-on boner.

*Think about something non-sexual. Think about your grandma. No, that's weird.*

Romy has been quiet so long that I'm wondering if she fell asleep.

But as if she can read my mind, she adjusts in her chair.

Without looking my way, she says, "Do you want to get in the water for a bit?"

"Whatever you want, sweetheart."

Now, she looks over at me. "Has anyone ever told you how sweet you are?"

*She probably wouldn't be thinking I'm so sweet if she knew what I was just thinking about doing to her tits.*

*Great. Now, I'm thinking about them again.*

She stands up and stretches. "Come on. Let's go swim. I'm sweating my boobs off."

*Dear Lord, I can't get away from them—not that I want to.*

I adjust my trunks in an attempt to keep everything contained before standing up to follow her into the water.

Once she's up to her waist, she quickly dives under the choppy surface to get used to it faster. When she comes back up, her nipples are hard and testing the limits of her top. I try not to stare, but I suck at playing it cool.

"See something you like, Boss Man?" Romy asks, tugging on the strings that hold everything together.

I want nothing more than to rip it off of her right now, but out of the corner of my eye, I see a few stragglers making their way to the beach. I'm guessing Romy doesn't want to show them her tits.

She walks toward me, working her bottom lip between her teeth. Droplets of water bead all over her fair skin, and the sun reflects off of every one of them.

I tell myself I'm going to behave. Romy doesn't want people getting the wrong idea about our working relationship. I respect that, so I'm not going to start pawing at her like an animal—not that I don't want to.

As she gets closer to me with that sex-kitten look in her eyes, though, I feel my resolve starting to weaken.

When she reaches me, her hand brushes against my cock beneath the water. It could have been mistaken as an accident—if I didn't see the look on her face as she did it.

She knows *exactly* what she's doing.

"Romy," I warn. "There are other people on this beach who can see our every move. I don't want to do anything that would make you feel uncomfortable."

"I'm not uncomfortable," she assures. "And I don't care who's watching."

She touches my dick again—this time, squeezing it and make her desires known.

Grabbing her waist, I pull her toward me until her body is firmly pressed against mine. My mouth crashes down on hers—kissing her like it's the last time.

Her lips part for me, and our tongues dance together. My dick is standing at full attention now, and it presses into her stomach. When it twitches against her, she moans into my mouth. Her teeth nip at my bottom lip, and I want nothing more than to slide into her and fuck her senseless right now. But I'll be damned if I let anyone else hear the noises she makes as she comes.

That's just for me—for the rest of the week anyway.

I reach under the water, and each of my hands grabs one of her juicy ass cheeks. The waves crash against us, but neither one of us seem to mind—or even notice.

Something seems to get Romy's attention, though, because she abruptly pulls back from our kiss.

"What's wrong?" I ask. "Are you okay?"

She looks up at me with wide eyes. "Something touched my foot."

"Well, sweetheart, it's the ocean. It's probably just a fish."

"I guess," she mutters as if trying to convince herself more than me. It's not working, though, because she's still frantically looking around.

"Do you want to go back up on the beach?" I ask.

"No. No, I'm fine." She shakes her head, forcing herself to calm down.

She leans up to kiss me, but before our lips can touch, she jumps once again.

"Holy shit, it touched me again!" She cries.

I look around us and see a small fin breaking the surface of the water. My heartbeat quickens, but I try to hide it as not to freak out Romy.

But it's too late.

She's already high-tailing it straight out of the water, holding onto her boobs as she attempts to run.

"You told me there weren't sharks!" She calls to me.

My eyes move back toward the fin, which is now moving closer. But suddenly, a blowhole pokes out of the water, spraying a gust of air.

It's not a shark—it's a damn dolphin.

I try calling after Romy to tell her that, but she either doesn't hear me or just doesn't care because she's still heading for land.

This whole thing has made my dick go back into hibernation, so I start to follow her—but without the rush.

I'm walking at a normal pace until I hear Romy cry out

again. She's grabbing her foot in pain. Now, I start mimicking her awkward run until I get to her.

"What happened?" I ask when I reach her.

"I think I stepped on something and cut my foot," she says, trying to balance on one foot to show me.

"Let's get you out of the water," I say, leading her to the beach.

When we get to the sand, I see the slight cut bleeding like a son-of-a-bitch.

"Okay, let's rinse it off one more time in the water, so we don't get sand in it," I tell her, helping her dip her foot back in the ocean.

She lets out a little shriek as the saltwater hits the exposed wound. "Boss Man, I don't know if you have noticed, but there's sand literally everywhere, and we left our shoes upstairs."

"I'm aware."

"So, I don't think we can avoid sand getting into—"

Before she can finish her thought, I lift her into my arms and start to carry her toward the path leading inside.

It doesn't take long for her to say, "Okay, I know I'm heavy. Your arms must be killing you."

"You're not heavy, baby," I reassure.

Once we are through the doors of the resort, she offers to walk three different times on the way back to her room. I say no every time and don't put her back on her feet until we are in the bathroom.

"You didn't have to do that," she scoffs as I take a look at her foot.

The bleeding has almost stopped, and once I wipe it off with a rag, I see it's not too bad.

"And you don't have to take care of me," she insists. "I'm fine."

"I know you are, but I'm going to take care of you anyway. Deal with it."

"Is that an order, Boss Man?" She says with a sly smile.

"Damn right it is. Now, hold still."

I quickly search the bathroom and find a small first aid kit in one of the drawers. Rifling through it, I pull out some cotton pads and hydrogen peroxide.

I dab a small amount of liquid onto the cotton and rub it on Romy's cut. She sucks in the air between her teeth as the peroxide stings.

"You okay?" I ask.

She nods, and I finish cleaning it out.

Looking it over, I say, "Well, I think you'll be able to keep the leg."

"Thanks, Doctor," she smiles. "Now, I have some other areas that could use a thorough exam and treatment."

She pulls me close to her and starts peppering kisses along my neck.

"Slow down, sweetheart. We've got all night."

She pouts out her bottom lip, but I just walk over to the large bathtub and start running some warm water. There's a small bottle of bubble bath with the other toiletries, so I add that in as well.

Turning my attention back to her, I untie the strings of her bikini and let it fall to the floor. My eyes roam over every inch of her, but I try to keep my dick at bay.

I'm trying to be sweet here.

I take her hand and lead her into the warm water. She gets comfortable in the tub, and I head out into the other room to try to find something to drink. The only thing left in the small refrigerator is some leftover beer. I could call room service, but they take forever.

*Beer it is.*

I pull out one of the bottles and walk back to the bathroom. When I enter, Romy is stretched out in the tub. The water is high enough now that the only things sticking out are her head, the tops of her breasts, and her toes.

She leans up just long enough to shut the water off before leaning back to get comfortable once more.

I hand her the bottle. "Sorry, beer was all we had, but if you want, I can order something else."

"Beer is just fine." She smiles before taking a swig.

"How's your foot?"

"That's just fine too. But I do have one problem that I need your help with."

I sit on the edge of the tub. "What's that?"

"I'm *very* lonely, and this bathtub is too big for me to be in all by myself."

"Is that right?" I can't help but smile.

She nods excitedly.

"I'm trying to let you relax," I say.

"Don't make me pull you in here with your shorts still on. I don't want to, but I'll do it."

The way she looks at me with those gorgeous eyes makes all of my resolve go right out the window, so I step out of my shorts and climb in the tub to join her.

# Chapter Nineteen

## ROMY

I scoot forward so that Aiden can climb in the water behind me. Neither one of us is exceptionally small, but we both fit perfectly in the oversized tub.

Once he's situated, I lean back against him. There's something so natural about being in his arms. I'm not quite sure what it is, but tt probably has to do with the fact that he's the sweetest man I've ever met.

And he has a filthy mouth. Is there really any better combination? It baffles me that he's still single. He told me all about Jane, but that was just one failed relationship. Have there been more? Why would anyone walk away from this man? I'll only have him for a week, but it will be hard as hell to give him up.

Aiden pulls me out of my thoughts when he asks, "What are you thinking about, beautiful?"

"You," I answer honestly.

He kisses the back of my shoulder. "What about me?"

"How I just can't wrap my head around how a great guy like you is still single."

"I told you about Jane and everything that happened. What else do you want to know?"

"Well, you said you've been with five women. If you take away Jane, that's still four women. Tell me about them."

His fingers lightly rub up and down my arms as he begins

to speak. "The first was in high school. We dated off and on for a couple of years, and it was fun, but neither one of us had a clue about what we were doing."

"The others were before I opened the business. Usually, the relationship would start in the summer when I wasn't doing classes, so we'd be able to spend a ton of time together. Then, classes would start back up again, and I'd get busy. It would all just fall apart."

He takes a deep breath and sighs before going on. I feel his chest rising and falling behind me.

"Romy, I wish I could tell you that I have a string of failed relationships through no fault of my own. But the truth is that my business seems to come first. It's like it's my first love, and any other relationship I have is like my mistress. At least, that's how it was for quite a while."

"And what about now?" I ask.

"Well, thanks to my amazing co-worker," he pauses to kiss my shoulder again. "I don't have as much to do, and the business runs a little more smoothly. Maybe I could make a relationship work now, but I don't know."

I'm a little taken back that he called me his 'co-worker.' I've always just been his assistant. But I figure it's probably just a slip of the tongue.

"For what it's worth," I begin. "I think you'll make some woman very happy someday."

He chuckles. "Thank you. For now, I'll settle for making you happy for the rest of the week."

"Oh, you are *definitely* doing that, Boss Man. In fact, that's what got me wondering why you haven't been snatched off the market yet."

"Well, now you know. But one thing I've learned is to make the most of the time we have."

We are quiet for a few minutes as he gets some soap on his hand and rubs it all over my skin. I do the same to him, making sure to take a little extra time to focus on his manhood. I feel it beginning to harden in my palm, but he stops me.

"The water is getting cold. Let's go get in bed."

"Lie on your stomach," he commands.

"Ohhh," I moan in excitement.

With a quiet laugh, he says, "Calm down, beautiful. We'll get there. I'm taking my time."

I crawl on the bed, letting my knees sink into the soft mattress. Once my head reaches the pillows, I lie down on my stomach as he instructed.

It takes Aiden a moment to join me, and when he does, I hear the top of some sort of bottle open. Seconds later, I feel his hands touch my skin. They're slick with what feels like lotion.

He starts at my shoulders and begins to work his way down, focusing on releasing the tension in every inch of my body. His fingers work their magic until I'm practically a puddle on the bed.

I'm in a complete state of relaxation—so much so that when he has me flip over, I don't even get turned on when he focuses his massage on my boobs.

Once he has rubbed every inch of me, I try to rally enough energy to move them into sexy time.

But my eyes are so heavy I can barely open them. And when I feel Aiden pull the blankets up over my body and crawl in bed next to me, I give up the good fight.

Before I drift off to sleep, though, I make a promise that tomorrow, I'm going to take care of him as wonderfully as he took care of me tonight.

Except dirtier.

Much dirtier.

# Chapter Twenty

## AIDEN

*A*nother day, another seminar I'm not paying attention to.
Maybe I should be saying *another day, another seminar filled with thoughts of Romy.*

Although my dick was upset it didn't get to play last night, the rest of me didn't mind. For some reason, I feel the inexplicable need to take care of Romy, which is ridiculous because I'm under no delusions that she needs anyone to take care of her. She's been taking care of herself for years now.

Yet, I still somehow want to do it. I want to hold her in my arms and tell her she doesn't have to face this world alone anymore. I want to say to her that she won't have to worry about a single thing as long as I'm around.

All this sunshine must be getting to me because I sound insane. Romy has always been just my assistant, and then, we get to Florida, and suddenly, I think I'm the man to make all of her dreams come true?

Maybe she's got a magical pussy—or maybe it has been too long since I've been inside one.

*Or maybe I finally realize exactly how special of a woman Romy is.*

I run my hand through the hair on my cheek, thinking about how entirely screwed I am—because I'm falling for a woman who wants this whole thing to only last a week. A week and then we go back to our everyday lives.

At the end of the day, Romy and I have an expiration date.

I may not like it, but it's the truth, so I just have to enjoy the week and then forget about it.

I'm pulled from my pity party when I feel my phone vibrate in my pocket. Typically, I wouldn't have even looked at it, but I see half the other people in the room are doing the same thing, so fuck it.

When I pull it out, I see Romy's name with a text underneath it.

**Romy: I took your advice, Boss Man.**

My forehead wrinkles as I try to figure out what she's talking about. I see three tiny dots appear on the screen, so I wait for her next message. Trying to be patient is agony.

But when it pops through, I see it was well worth the wait.

**Romy: I decided not to wear any panties today.**

I try to play it cool as I text back, but I can feel my dick already threatening to make an appearance.

**Me: Oh yeah? I'm glad you're finally listening.**

It doesn't take long for her to reply.

**Romy: Yeah, I kind of like it. It's very...breezy—especially since I'm wearing such a short sundress.**

*Jesus.*

When I saw her in that cute dress this morning, I was already thinking about bending her over and fucking her senseless. Her not wearing anything underneath makes that idea even more appealing.

When I get lost in my thoughts about burying myself in her tight pussy, she texts again.

**Romy: The only problem is that it's a little uncomfortable with how wet I am.**

*Sweet baby Jane, she's driving me insane.*

**Me: Why are you so wet, sweetheart?**

**Romy: Thinking about you...inside of me. Maybe I'll just head upstairs and take care of the problem myself.**

**Me: Oh, no the fuck you won't. I'm leaving this class now.**

**Meet me upstairs.**

I quietly stand up and head for the door, grateful that I picked a seat near the back of the large room.

I swear this woman is making me crazy. One minute, I want to be sweet and take care of her, and the next, I'm chomping at the bit to rip off all her clothes and make her come over and over again.

But I guess in a way, that's taking care of her too, isn't it? And for the next few days, I think that's the *perfect* way to take care of her.

As I make my way upstairs, I pull out my phone and fire off one more text to my little sex goddess.

**Me: And sweetheart, don't keep me waiting.**

# Chapter Twenty-one

## ROMY

After getting the text from Aiden to not keep him waiting, I have to stop myself from sprinting upstairs.

After skipping the sex last night, I was determined to make up for it today. Feeling bold, I decided to go sans underwear—which is so entirely unlike me.

What can I say? The man brings it out in me.

I waited as long as I could before sending him the teasing texts. We made it through almost an entire day of classes before I caved. I feel bad that he keeps skipping things for me, so I tried to be good.

But there was something so deliciously tempting about making sure he was thinking about me when he was supposed to be doing something else.

A little payback for all the time I spend thinking about him.

And now, he's upstairs waiting to do filthy things to my body.

And maybe it's just me, but this elevator is going slower than it ever has before.

As I stand alone in the big metal box, I ponder what Aiden might do to me. The thoughts give me butterflies.

But if I'm being honest with myself, it's not just the sex stuff that has my stomach doing somersaults. It's Aiden in general. Just the thought of being around him gives me that warm, fuzzy feeling.

Maybe it's my denial, but I tell myself it's the fact that I know I'm about to have some orgasms. I refuse to believe it's more than that.

The elevator doors finally open, and I step off, hurrying toward my room. I assume that's where he'll be.

When I reach the door, I take a deep breath before sticking my key in the reader. Once the light turns green, I push inside.

My eyes scan the room for Aiden, but it takes me a moment to spot him out on the balcony. He's leaned back in one of the chairs with one leg stretched out in front of him. He's wearing dark blue jeans with a casual white button-up shirt—the top few buttons are undone, falling open to expose his chest.

He's sipping on a beer as he looks out over the ocean. Damn, he's a whole lot of man.

I slide the glass door open and join him on the balcony. He looks up at me and smiles.

"No panties, huh?" He asks, raising his eyebrows.

My shoulders shrug as I feign innocence. "I just decided to take your advice."

He reaches up and takes ahold of my hand, gently pulling me toward him. He guides me so that I'm sitting in his lap.

He takes the bottle in his hand and sets it on the ground before bringing me toward him for a kiss. I can still taste the beer on his tongue as it swirls with mine.

I feel his large hand stroke up and down my thigh, and I'm grateful that I didn't stop my shaving at the thigh today.

When his lips pull back from mine, his hand moves further North as he says, "Are you really not wearing any panties?"

Feeling bold, I say, "Why don't you find out for yourself?"

It's as though a switch flips, and his eyes turn lustful and hungry. They stare at me like they *need* me.

His hand moves even further up until his fingers are close enough to tease my slit. I feel him run his fingers through my wetness, making sure to add extra pressure to my clit.

"Is that pussy wet for me, baby?" He whispers against my skin.

His dirty talk makes me even wetter.

I nod and let out a quiet moan as he slips a finger inside, toying with that special spot.

My arms clench around Aiden's neck as he continues to rub my g-spot while his thumb plays with my clit.

My fingers dig into his shoulders as he ramps me up. Every nerve in my body is screaming to life. Pleasure runs through my veins like wildfire flows through a forest.

But just when I'm about to chase my orgasm over the edge into a state of euphoria, he stops and pulls his hand out.

Licking my juices off his fingers, he says, "It's not nice to tease—is it?"

"Please," I moan.

Usually, I'd never beg, but damn, my clit is pulsing, and I need to come.

"Please, what?" He asks.

"Please make me come."

"Stand up," he commands.

I start to pout until I see what he's got in mind. He unzips his jeans and pulls out his thick cock. He pulls the denim down just enough to expose his manhood but nothing else.

He reaches for my hand and leads me back to him, positioning me so I'm facing away from him and looking out over the waves.

I feel his fingers on my hips as they lower me onto him. I'm already so wet that he slides into me with ease.

I gasp as he fills and stretches me in the best way imaginable.

Once he's fully inside, we are still for a moment before he commands, "Ride me, baby. Do what makes you feel good."

I start slow—at first grinding on him before beginning to bounce up and down. I lay my hands on his thighs to give me more leverage.

It feels incredible, but I'll admit that I'm not exactly in the best *dick-riding* shape. So, soon my legs start to get tired.

But Aiden comes to the rescue.

He leans up so that he's sitting upright. One of his hands slips under my cotton dress and works its way to where our bodies are joined. I spread my legs wider, giving him complete access.

His fingers zone in on my clit and start to work their magic. He uses his other hand to grab my hip and continue to move me up and down.

He starts talking to me in a low tone. "Do you like that, baby? Do you like looking down there at the beach and knowing that at any moment, someone could look up here and see me fucking you? They could see me buried in your pussy."

Realistically, I know we are probably too high up for anyone to really be able to tell what we are doing, but the thought of someone watching us turns me on even more.

And Aiden talking dirty about it? Good lord, my vagina is like a dang waterfall it's so turned on.

"Look at you, sweetheart. You fucking love it," he says.

I moan as we both start to increase our tempos.

"Come for me," he commands, applying more pressure to my clit. "Let all those people watch what I do to you."

The combination of his fingers and filthy mouth is enough to send me flying over the edge. My whole body starts to shake as the waves of my orgasm crash over me like the waves of the ocean down below.

I start to cry out, but Aiden's hand covers my mouth.

"Sorry, sweetheart. No one besides me gets to hear that," he growls.

I ride out my orgasm for what feels like forever, and when my body finally calms, he commands, "Come on, let's go back inside."

I stand up, and he slides out of me. Missing that full feeling already, I hurry back inside the room. Before I can lie on the bed, he stops me. He is instead positioning me, so I'm on my hands and knees. Leaning forward, I follow the rule, 'face down, ass up,' which gives him the perfect view of my big butt.

"Damn baby, look at you," he admires while running his hands along my round cheeks.

He lines up his cock with my entrance, but I feel a light slap on my backside before pushing forward.

It hurts for a split second, but then it turns into something else—something I want him to do again. When I back my ass up toward him, he must get the point because as he starts fucking me, he gives it a couple more slaps.

His fingers grip my hips as he moves in and out of me. This angle lets him go impossibly deep, and it's fucking incredible.

Doggy style has always been a favorite of mine, but this is on a whole other level. I'm still so sensitive from my last orgasm that every movement feels even more intense.

Aiden moves harder and faster as we both hurtle toward the finish line. My clit begs for attention, so I reach between my legs to rub it.

I know it won't take long, and when Aiden says, "Yeah, baby, come again for me. Let me feel it," it's enough to finish the job.

I tighten around him, and this time, I don't have to be quiet. My lungs get a workout as I cry out his name. He holds out as long as possible, but it doesn't take long for him to finish.

When we're done, I head to the bathroom to pee and clean myself up. Despite my legs feeling like jelly, I manage to make it there okay.

When I come back, I see Aiden lying in bed, the blankets only covering him from the waist down.

He's taken his hair down, and it covers his shoulders and part of his chest.

He's so damn sexy—even more so when he sees me and smiles.

I join him on the bed, and he pulls me close.

"Are you okay?" He asks.

My eyes glance up at him. "You just fucked my brains out. Why wouldn't I be okay?"

"That's my point," he says. "I know I can get a bit rough sometimes, so I want you to tell me if I ever take it too far."

I never thought about it like that. Sure, it was a little rough, but I didn't think it was too much. Truth is...I kind of liked it.

Okay, the truth is...I *really* liked it.

But it's sweet of him to worry about me.

I lay my hand on his face and rub my thumb through his beard.

"You weren't too rough. I loved it."

"You sure?"

I nod. "I'm sure. Aiden, I've got some meat on me. You can be rough—I'm not going to break."

He smiles a wickedly sexy grin. "Oh, I'm sure that gorgeous body of yours can handle it. I just don't want to do anything to make you feel uncomfortable."

"Never," I reassure.

He kisses the top of my head and pulls me close. I curl up against his body as his large arms wrap around me. At this moment, the fact that we are boss and assistant is a million miles away.

It feels more like we are an actual couple, which is ridiculous because this entire thing is temporary.

But there's a small part of me that wishes it wasn't.

Once again...ridiculous.

I try to lighten the mood and stop feeling...however it is that I'm feeling.

I laugh and say, "So, do you think that the old couple we keep running into saw us banging on the balcony?"

# Chapter Twenty-two

## AIDEN

"Oh, you did *not* just say that," Romy scolds with her eyes wide and her finger pointed at me.

"Hey, I'm just being honest," I begin, but she cuts me off.

"Aiden Montgomery, you're saying you *liked* Star Wars Episodes 1-3?!" Her voice is a few octaves higher than usual.

"Romy, I didn't say they were my favorite movies ever, and clearly 4-6 are way better. I'm just saying that I don't think they deserve as much hate as I always get," I try to defend.

She still looks as though I've just kicked her puppy.

She points her finger at me again. "Just because your face looks like that doesn't mean it can say crazy things."

"You think my face looks good?" I smile and wiggle my eyebrows up and down.

"Yes, but that's not the point, Aiden."

"What *is* the point?"

"Haven't you been listening?" She shrieks. "The first three Star Wars movies are awful!"

Reaching for the remote, she declares, "That's it. We are going to watch the original three just so that *maybe* you can come to your senses."

I hold my hands up in defeat. "Okay, okay. Whatever you want."

"Oh, soon you will agree with me, Mr. Montgomery."

My dick twitches hearing her call me that. After she called me that when she was naked, it's firmly fixed in my brain. When we go home, she might just have to forever call me Aiden—if she doesn't want me to bend her over her desk.

I glance at the clock. "So, you want to start a Star Wars marathon at almost nine at night?"

"Sir, we will stay up all damn night until you learn your lesson."

She flips through the TV menu until she comes to the search engine. She types in the title, and it pops up on the screen.

Now, my voice is the one that goes up a couple of notches. "Twelve dollars to rent a movie?!"

She glares at me. "Take it out of my paycheck."

"You know I'm not going to do that," I say. "Just commenting on the resort being money-hungry."

I really don't care about the price, but it's a little cute watching her get all worked up—especially over something nerdy like Star Wars. The truth is that I would pay a hundred dollars for it just to make her happy.

Besides, we've had a long day, and it'll be nice to relax.

We were good students today and made it to all of our classes, and afterward, there was a dinner they put on for everyone that we went to. Mingling with other people you don't know is something we typically both avoid, but a prime rib dinner was a little hard to turn down.

We got a couple of side-eyed looks from people questioning exactly what our relationship was, but when we kept everything 100% professional, everyone seemed to chill out. Well, it was professional until I felt Romy running her hand up my thigh until she got to the prize she was looking for.

Thank the lord for long white tablecloths that hid our activities from prying eyes.

Romy charmed everyone with her charm and wit. She may think that she's awkward, but it didn't show tonight—all while teasing me under the table.

After dinner, I immediately brought her back upstairs to teach her a dirty little lesson. I love how frisky she is.

We only have two more days in paradise, and I'd be lying if I said I was ready for it to end. I've been savoring every second we've had together because I know when we go home, it all goes away.

Hell, I wanted to skip classes today and go to the beach, but Romy insisted we go try to learn some stuff.

And tomorrow is the seminar I'm speaking at, so we won't be able to miss it. That leaves us Friday. There's a closing ceremony earlier in the day and another dinner, but I have other plans—plans for just us.

My eyes glance over at her, and she's staring at the screen as though it's the first time she's ever laid eyes on Star Wars.

It's cute.

My little nerd.

Well, not *my* little nerd—although I'd like her to be.

Even though I've pictured it a few times, now is truly the first time I'm admitting it to myself.

I wouldn't mind—no fuck that.

I *want* a relationship with Romy after this week ends. I'd love to be able to say that she's all mine.

Mentally, I'm thinking about how I can convince her to still be with me when we land in Minnesota.

She pulls me from my thoughts when she gets up to head for the bathroom. She reaches for the towel she had wrapped around her hair earlier and pulls it around her body.

I don't say anything to her as she walks away from me, but when she's done and walking back toward me, I say, "What's with the towel?"

Looking down at the terrycloth material, she replies, "Didn't want all my jiggly parts hanging out."

"First of all, I *like* those jiggly parts. And second, I have seen you naked so many times this week. I've stared at every inch of you. Hell, I've even seen your butt hole, and now, you want to get self-conscious? Baby, how many times do I have to say it?"

Her eyes narrow in on me as a line in the middle of her forehead appears. "Hold on...when did you examine my butt hole?"

I laugh. "Romy, I didn't *examine* it, but you understand that when you bend over for me to fuck you from behind, it's just sort of right there—on display."

She looks mortified. "No, I most certainly did not realize that."

"Baby, it's not a big deal." I smile at her. "Don't make me bend you over right now and show you."

She still looks skeptical and surprises me when she asks, "Are you one of those guys who is obsessed with butt sex?"

"What?"

"It seems like every guy I've been with has always asked me over and over again when they get to put it in my ass."

"And it never occurred to you that they're able to see your butt hole during sex?" I ask.

She still looks confused, so I go on. "But to answer your question, I wouldn't say I'm obsessed with it. If a woman wants to do it, I'm up for it. I'll do anything she wants, but I'm okay with not doing it too. For me, the pussy is the main event."

"You really are the perfect man, aren't you?"

I can't help but laugh. "Not even close, but I'm glad you think so."

"Have you ever done it?" She asks in a more hushed tone.

"Done what?"

"Anal sex."

I knew what she was talking about, but I wanted to see the cute blush creep up her cheeks as she said it.

"Once," I reply. "The woman I was seeing wanted to experiment with it."

She simply nods.

"Have you tried it?" I ask.

Now, her head shakes back and forth. "Nope. I mean, I wouldn't be against trying it sometime. I never felt comfortable enough with any of the guys I've been with to ever do it."

"And comfort and trust are a huge part of it. You have to be completely at ease with the person you're doing it with," I say.

I'm tempted to tell her that if she wants to try it, I'd be happy to guide her through it. But I highly doubt we will be doing anal play before we head back to Minnesota.

We sit in an awkward silence for a few moments before I try to lighten the subject a little.

"Now, before you changed the subject, I was trying to tell you how you don't need the towel to cover up anything on your sexy body—jiggly or not."

She rolls her eyes as if she still doesn't believe me. "Maybe I wouldn't mind the jiggle so much if it wasn't accompanied by the cellulite and stretch marks."

Grabbing her hand, I put it on my stomach. "Feel that? Jiggly? I don't have six-pack abs, and you still think I'm attractive, right?"

"Duh."

"And feel this." I move her hand to my side right above my hip.

Her eyes move toward where our hands are. "Stretch marks?" She asks.

I nod. "Did you even notice them before I showed you right now?"

She gives me a slight smile. "There are far more things to look at on you than stretch marks."

Using my finger to pull her chin toward me, I press my lips lightly to hers. I think I'll miss kissing her most of all. Her lips are so damn soft.

When we break apart, I say, "Back at you, baby."

# Chapter Twenty-three

## ROMY

"Are you sure you're not nervous?" I ask Aiden for about the fourth time. "You'll be standing up in front of all those people."

Aiden looks down at me as we stand shoulder to shoulder in the elevator. "Romy, do you *want* me to be nervous? Because I wasn't, but you're making it sound terrifying."

I lay my hand on my chest, gesturing to myself. "I'm just saying that if it were me, I'd be nervous talking to a room full of people like that."

His shoulders shrug as he shoves his hands in his pockets. "I guess it would be different if it were a topic I knew nothing about, but I'm talking about my business--the most important thing in the world to me. If I'm comfortable talking about anything, it's that."

Why does it slightly hurt my feelings that he called his business the most important thing in his life?

*Because I'm insane. That's why.*

This man and I don't have an actual relationship. We have a —well, I don't know what we have.

A Florida Fling?

An ocean-side orgasm party?

A seven-day sexcapade?

My lips crease tightly as I try to stifle my laughter at how funny I am inside my own head.

Aiden notices. "What's so funny?"

"Uh, nothing. Just thinking about that whole picturing everyone in their underwear thing," I lie.

He turns toward me, so his large body is against mine. His presence is one that demands to be felt.

When he leans down to whisper, I get goosebumps everywhere. "Trust me, Romy, you're the *only* one I'll be picturing in her underwear." Leaning in even closer, he adds, "Maybe even nothing at all."

I feel like I'm about to melt into a puddle at this man's feet, so I decide to return the favor.

My tongue pokes out and glides along my bottom lip as my eyes flick up at him. "Well, I guess it's a good thing I'm not wearing any underwear again, huh?"

He forms a fist and brings it to his mouth, biting his knuckles.

He lets out a low growl before saying, "I swear if we weren't so pressed for time, I'd take you back upstairs and have you hike up that dress and sit on my face."

"There's always later," I tease.

"And believe me, you *are* on the menu later," he promises.

*Damn, this man has me coming apart without even touching me.*

The elevator doors open, and we try to exit as though we weren't mere seconds away from ripping each other's clothes off.

Side-by-side, we walk to the conference hall. Outside the door, there's a sign that reads:

**HOW TO GET YOUR BUSINESS OFF THE GROUND**

And Aiden is listed under one of the guest speakers.

When we walk in, the room is still filling up as groups of people stand around and talk amongst themselves.

We head toward the front of the room, where the podium sits upon a slightly raised stage.

Aiden leads me to a chair in the front row that is marked with a **RESERVED** sign.

"This is all you, sweetheart," he says, removing the sign.

But only one seat is reserved. "What about you?" I ask.

He points to the stage, and I see a table with a few chairs. "I have to sit there. After we each speak, they will do a short panel where people can ask questions."

I nod. Although I wish he was sitting next to me, at least he will be some good eye candy to gawk at.

It's only a few minutes before the moderator comes in to get things started. Everyone takes a seat, and the man gives a short introduction.

After he's done, the first speaker walks to the podium. He's a rugged-looking man who is probably in his mid-fifties.

His speech is all about how he used powerful marketing and advertising to grow his business. He spent years in a rut before it finally took off, and now, he's netting six figures a year.

The second speaker is much younger and discusses the magic of social media and blah, blah, blah. Honestly, he seems a little full of himself.

Next up is Aiden, and I swear I feel nervous for him. But if he's the least bit anxious, it doesn't show. He looks completely at ease.

The microphone makes an ugly high-pitched squeal as he begins talking, but it doesn't seem to phase him.

"Good afternoon. My name is Aiden Montgomery, and I'm the founder, owner, and sometimes, the grunt man for Montgomery Construction." That gets a small laugh out of the crowd.

"I wish that I could stand up here and give you some magic formula to make your business take off. I wish there were a magic button you could press to make you rich, but there's not. There's just blood, sweat, and tears—and a hell of a lot of hard work."

"When I first started my business, every penny I had that didn't go toward cheap food like instant noodles went toward paying for my business. I was sleeping in my childhood bedroom in my parent's house to save on rent. I was taking small jobs that I could do by myself since I couldn't afford to hire anyone yet."

He pauses for a moment, rubbing his beard as he thinks.

Taking a deep breath, he continues, "I'm not going to stand here and sugar coat things and tell you it's going to be easy. It's not. You'll have to make sacrifices you never imagined.

"I'm also not going to stand up here and bullshit you. Honestly, I was surprised when I was asked to speak at this conference because I don't feel like I've done anything awe-inspiring. Yes, I have built a successful business, but it took years and a ton of work. And I didn't do it entirely alone.

"As I said, I had *very* supportive and understanding parents who let me come back home, so I could save money. I have a fantastic crew—some of which came to work for me when I could barely pay them minimum wage.

"And then, there's my assistant." He pauses again, and I feel myself gasp.

He goes on, "I use that word, but honestly, she hasn't been my assistant for a while. She walked in with her business degree in hand, and when I took the time to listen, she gave me a full-blown presentation on all the things I was doing wrong. At first, I didn't know how to take it, but when I put my ego aside, I realized she was right. Truth be told, my business wouldn't be what it is today without her.

"My point is that you should accept help when it's given. And when it *is* given, show how much it's appreciated."

Aiden turns and looks right at me before adding, "Sometimes you don't know how wonderful it is until it's staring at you right in the face."

Hearing his words brings up all of the emotion I've been trying to shove down all week. The man I've always look at as my grumpy boss is looking at me with the same sentiment that I'm feeling.

This week, I've realized just how much of a good man he is —a man that I would be lucky to call mine. I've dated enough of the bad ones to know a good one when I see it.

And Aiden Montgomery might just be one of the best.

We've only been here for a week, but there's something

real brewing between the two of us. That makes me happier than I've ever been, yet simultaneously terrifies me.

Because he's still my boss.

And everything could end *very* badly.

But I can't deny the fact that I find myself quickly, and very deeply, falling in love with him.

# Chapter Twenty-four

## ROMY

This time, our trip in the elevator is a bit quieter than our ride earlier in the day.

I spent the rest of the seminar with my head in a fog. Aiden's words hit me right in the feels, and I can't stop thinking about them. They replay in my head as I try to decipher their exact meaning and tone.

Was it just a boss telling his employee how much she's appreciated? That's probably what it looked like to everyone else.

But to me, it seemed like more—so much more. Maybe I'm reading too much into things. I might be imagining all of it.

The thing I'm not imagining? The way I felt about him when he said it.

And now, we are once again trapped in this elevator. The air is thick with all of the things we yearn to say to one another. Neither one of us utters a word the entire ride, but when I feel Aiden's fingers entwine with mine, somehow all of the tension just seems to disappear.

When the doors slide open, we step out and walk down the hall, holding hands the entire way.

When we walk into my room—or *our* room as it's come to be—I toss my purse onto the bed and start to walk to the tiny fridge to grab a water bottle.

But Aiden pulls on my hand, bringing me back to him.

"Hey," he says in a quiet tone. "Are you okay? You haven't said a word since we left the seminar. Did something I say upset you?"

"No!" I exclaim. "Not at all. I loved what you said. It feels good to be—appreciated."

"Then, what's wrong?" His thumb strokes over my cheek, and I try to hold back the waves of emotion threatening to bust through the dam.

"I just never expected any of this to happen. When you asked me to come with you on this trip, I thought it would be just like work—which is fine. I like my job. But when we got here, everything changed. It wasn't like work at all. And you're so... fucking perfect."

He chuckles, but I keep talking. "And somehow here in Key West—with you—I'm not nearly so awkward. It's like you make me feel totally different. And you're my boss, so I'm just not sure what to make of any of it."

I'm full-on rambling now, but I just can't seem to stop. "And then, you get up there on that stage and say all those things, and I don't know what to make of any of that either—"

In an attempt to shut me up, Aiden presses his lips to mine. His kiss makes me lose any train of thought I just had.

When he pulls back to look at me, he says, "Will you hush for a minute?"

Since my ability to speak seems to have gone right out the window, I just give a quick nod. He looks down as he takes both of my hands in his and then takes a deep breath before beginning to speak.

"Romy, I never expected any of this to happen either. As your boss, I was pretty sure you hated me. Despite that, you have done more for my business than I ever thought possible. And I don't think I ever expressed to you how much it's genuinely appreciated.

My heart sinks a little, listening to him only talk about our professional relationship.

But he isn't done.

"And all of that was before we even got here. You're right; when we came down here, something seemed to click, and I wish I could tell you what that means for us or where we go from here. But I don't have the answer. What I do know, though, is that you have become a very big—very important— part of my life, and I don't want to lose you."

He reaches his hand up to wipe away the lone tear that is now rolling down my cheek. "I'm crazy about you, Romy—in every way imaginable."

That's all I need to hear before I moan and he brings me toward him once again. This time, we don't immediately pull apart. This time, we stay locked in the moment—our lips touching as we melt into one another.

His tongue runs along the seam of my lips, seeking entrance. I grant it, and he deepens the kiss, his tongue beginning to dance with mine.

My arms wrap around his neck as my fingers run through his hair. I do everything I can to pull him even closer.

Aiden must get the message because he lays his hands on my hips, and in one swift motion, he pulls me onto his lap, so I'm straddling him.

I can feel the bulge in his pants growing larger as it presses into me. I made good on my promise not to wear panties, so I'm pretty sure I'm leaving a wet spot on the front of his jeans.

I'm too swept up in our kiss to care though. The way his tongue moves makes my head go all foggy.

His kiss has always been passionate, but this is filled with more emotion than ever before.

His lips leave mine for a moment. When he pulls back to look at me, he pushes the hair back from my face and tucks it behind my ear.

"Beautiful," he whispers, and I melt all over again.

He kisses me again, but this time, he lifts me and lays me down on the soft mattress before climbing on top of me.

His mouth moves from my lips down to my neck, finding the most sensitive spot. He kisses and nips at it, and my senses are completely overwhelmed with nothing but Aiden. From the feel of his lips to the way his hair lightly tickles me as it feathers across my skin. The way he smells like soap and cologne. The way his kiss somehow tastes like everything I've ever wanted.

When one hand moves to my breasts and tweaks my nipple through the material of my dress, my body comes to life. It feels good, but I yearn for more. My body *needs* more contact.

Aiden sits up on his knees and reaches his fingers up to my shoulders, grabbing the thin straps and pulling. Teasingly slowly, he brings the dress down my body. Once it's off, he focuses on doing the same to my bra.

Once I'm naked beneath his hungry gaze, he spends time focusing on each of my breasts, sucking each of my nipples into his mouth and licking over it with his tongue.

While his mouth gives attention to my chest, his hand slides between my legs, making sure I'm ready for him.

Feeling that I'm more than ready, he slides his cock inside with ease. I gasp at the feeling—the feeling I get every time he and I have sex.

Although there *is* something different about this time. There's always been passion and emotion, but this is more.

Something like, dare I say...love.

He moves inside me—every movement slow and deliberate. I wrap my arms around his neck, pulling him down to get lost in his kiss once again.

We lie there trapped in time—trapped in a moment. We make love and pour everything we have into each other.

He takes his time as we both build toward an explosive finish. I moan into his kiss as one of his hands reaches between us and rubs my clit.

Damn, the man handles it like a magic button because soon enough, I'm tightening around him and riding the waves of an epic orgasm.

My legs wrap around his back, pulling him even closer, and soon, he's coming inside me.

When we've finished, we snuggle up and fall into a comfortable silence. The gravity of what we just did hits me like a ton of breaks. This wasn't just sex or fucking—this was making love. This had all of our feelings toward each other come bubbling to the surface.

There's a part of me that wants to fall in bed like this every single night for the rest of our lives. But I know that's just not possible.

Is it?

# Chapter Twenty-five

## AIDEN

The following day, I'm up earlier than Romy—as usual—so I shower and head downstairs to get us some coffee. Before I make my way to the small cafe, I take a few minutes just to walk around and collect my thoughts.

Yesterday was—I don't even know what it was, but I know it was great.

I meant every word I said to Romy. I'm not sure if she knows my words go beyond the scope of the business, but I know that they do.

If I were to tell people that I fell in love with my assistant on a work trip, most would think it's just the sun, booze, or hormones.

But I'd say that they're wrong. Maybe those things helped to open my eyes, but I believe my feelings are entirely genuine. All those things helped me to see how fucking amazing Romy is.

And last night, something seemed to shift between us. I've always been a man who loves the rougher side of six. Don't get me wrong—I always make sure my woman is satisfied, but usually, I'm all for the animalistic passion and dirty talk.

Last night, though, all I wanted to do was take my time with Romy and make love to her. I wanted to show her how much she means to me.

It was nice even though it's not quite what I'm used to. It's like we were connected on an almost spiritual level.

*Good lord, that sounds sappy.*

*Oh well, fuck it. I'll be a sap for her.*

She and I still haven't talked about what happens when we leave our tropical paradise. Considering our flight leaves early tomorrow morning, we will have to have that conversation today.

And honestly, I have no idea how it's going to go.

If I had my way, I'd tell her how crazy I am about her. I'd ask her to be all mine no matter where we are—Key West, Minnesota, or the fucking moon. I don't care as long as we are together.

Yes, I want to tell her all of that, but I don't want to make her feel uncomfortable.

My feet carry me outside to the beach. I don't go down by the water but instead, take a seat on one of the nearby beach chairs.

The sun is still coming up over one end of the beach, and there's a nice breeze blowing off the water.

I lean back in the corner and cross my arms over my chest. As beautiful as this view is, all my mind can focus on is Romy.

What if I tell her all of this, and she doesn't feel the same way? And then consequently, our work relationship is ruined. I know what a fantastic asset she is to my company, and I don't want to lose her.

*It sounds awful when I say it like that.*

Damn! How am I going to handle all of this?

I run my hand over my beard and stare out over the water, trying to gain some type of clarity over this whole situation.

As much as I want to be with Romy, I figure I should let her dictate where we go from here. I decide to feel her out and figure out precisely what it is that she wants.

If she still wants to call it quits at the end of the week, we will. We can go back to our boss/assistant relationship. I'll never force her into something she doesn't want.

And if I'm right, she feels the same way I do, and all of this will be a moot point.

But the real question is—what do I do if I'm wrong?

# Chapter Twenty-six

## ROMY

**M**y eyes open to the sound of my phone ringing on the nightstand next to me. I reach over and grab it to look at the screen.

It takes a moment to focus, but when I do, I see Veronica's name. I figure it must be important for her to call the day before I'm due to come home.

Clearing my throat, I answer, "Hello?"

"Shit, I'm sorry, Romy. I didn't mean to wake you," Veronica says.

"It's fine. I'm up. What's going on?" I sit up and wipe some of the sleep out of my eyes.

"I didn't want to call, but I thought it was important."

"V, cut to the point," I snap, suddenly feeling a pit in my stomach starting to form.

"Well, when I went to your place to water the plants, someone stopped by to deliver some paperwork for you. I went ahead and signed for them, and you know I'm nosey…"

"Of course," I say. "Go on."

"You already know that I opened it and read the papers."

"And?" I'm losing patience.

"It's some paperwork about the feds filing charges against your father. They are calling you as a material witness."

Louder than I mean to, I cry, "What the hell for?"

"Apparently, they found his little off-shore bank accounts, and since all of that money was illegally obtained, they are charging him with new crimes for all of it. They've called you to testify against him," she says.

"Why would I have to testify? I haven't spoken to him in years!"

"Romy, the accounts were in your name. I imagine they think you have something to do with it."

*Son of a bitch.*

My blood boils, but I wish I were more surprised than I actually am. This is sort of par for the course with my father. He's still just as much of a piece of shit as he's always been.

"I've never touched any of that money. I don't even want it," I say.

"Yeah, Romy, we both know that, and it's easy enough to prove. But it might be a good idea to get a lawyer to keep on retainer until the whole thing is sorted out."

I know she's right, but that doesn't mean that I like it. Lawers are expensive, and I'm not exactly swimming in cash.

She continues, "I didn't want to call, but I didn't want you to come home and be blindsided either."

"No, I get it, V. Thanks for calling."

"Do you want me to scan the papers and email them to you?" She asks.

I lean back, propping myself up on one arm, and I feel something under my hand. My fingers pick up the small slip of paper, and I look it over.

**Coffee run...Be right back.**

**-A**

My mouth instantly curls into a smile at the mere thought of Aiden. Immediately, I'm filled with a pang of disappointment that it's our last day here.

The last day we can live in our little fantasy and pretend the rest of the world doesn't exist.

The last day I can pretend a man like Aiden Montgomery could be all mine.

I don't want to ruin our final day.

"Romy?" Veronica pulls me out of my thoughts.

"Sorry, I'm here—just a little overwhelmed, I guess. No, you don't have to email them. I'll just look at them when I get home."

"Okay. Can't wait to hear all about your trip."

We say our goodbyes, and I hang up the phone before wondering exactly how much I'll tell Veronica when I get home. Yes, she's my best friend, but this secret seems like it would be so much more special if it stayed between Aiden and I.

Maybe it should just stay a secret. Although I've been entertaining the idea of continuing this—whatever it is that we have—now, it seems like a horrible idea.

Sure, maybe it would be great for a while, but how often do you hear about a relationship between a boss and an assistant working out?

This isn't some Sandra Bullock Rom-Com.

And who always gets screwed in the equation? The assistant.

And I can't afford to lose my job—especially now that I'm probably going to have a big, fat bill from an attorney.

That's a whole other issue that I have no idea how to handle.

*I could always tell Aiden and get his opinion. Maybe even ask for his help.*

No. I've been doing it on my own for this long. I'm not about to stop now.

But to continue taking care of myself, I need to keep my job. And to do that, I need to keep things with my boss strictly professional.

After today, that is.

Last night, Aiden and I decided to play hookey from the conference one last time and spend the day together. I don't know what he has planned, but I do know that I don't want to ruin our time together with all of my drama.

I decide to take a shower to try to clear my mind for the

day ahead.

When I step under the hot water, I let it roll over my skin, picturing my worries going down the drain with the run-off.

I have no idea how long I'm standing there when I hear the shower door open.

I don't have to look back to know that it's Aiden. His presence is demanding enough to be felt.

Well, that…and he has a key.

His large arms wrap around me, and I lean back into him. In his arms might be the safest I've ever felt.

"Hey, baby," he whispers, pulling me tighter. His beard tickles my neck and cheek as he talks.

"Hey, Boss Man," I reply with a smile. "Didn't you already take a shower this morning?"

"Maybe." He kisses my cheek. "But I couldn't resist when you're in here all alone—and all wet and soapy."

"So, instead of coming in the shower to get clean, you came in to get dirty?"

He laughs, and I feel his cock twitch against my backside. "Well, I think you and I already concluded that maybe shower sex isn't the best idea, but I figured I could tease you enough to make you horny when we get out."

"You know it won't take very much convincing."

My head falls back against him as he starts to prove my point. Each of his large hands finds one of my breasts. His fingers are rough yet somehow soft at the same time as they tweak and tease my nipples. Sensations fire off, leading straight to my clit. It pulses between my legs, begging for contact.

As if he can read my mind, Aiden moves one of his hands downward. It slides along the slick skin straight to where I need it most.

I reach back, grabbing whatever my hands can reach as he rubs my clit in small circles. When he pulls the hood back and starts playing with the most sensitive part, my legs about collapse underneath me.

Aiden leans in to whisper, "Let's move this to the bed,

baby."

I frantically nod, and we both get out and dry off at lightning speed.

Aiden's the first one to the bed, so I decide to do a little teasing of my own.

I cross the room with my towel still wrapped around me. He's lying on the bed, his cock standing straight up. He strokes it a few times as I let my towel fall to the floor.

*Why is that so sexy?*

I get on the bed and crawl toward him. Instead of immediately climbing on his dick and bouncing on it like a pogo stick, I settle between his legs and take a firm grasp on his member.

I mimic what he did, stroking up and down, trying to do it the way he likes it. My small hand barely fits around the girth.

Without waiting too long, I angle it toward my mouth. My tongue flicks out as I lick all around the purple head.

Aiden grabs a pillow and props it behind his head to get a better view of what I'm doing. He groans as I close my mouth around him and take him as far down my throat as I can go—which honestly isn't too far.

Coke can, remember?

But I try my best, and Aiden certainly isn't complaining. No, he's muttering something incoherent while he runs his fingers through my hair.

Every once in a while I catch the words, "Fuck, baby," so I assume he's enjoying himself.

I keep going, changing up my speed and switching between licks and sucks—There's something about making Aiden lose his mind with pleasure that is a massive turn-on for me.

Just when I think he's about to blow in my mouth, he pulls me off of him.

"Give me some of that pussy, baby," he growls.

Good lord, his dirty talk is making me come undone before he's even inside me.

I straddle him and slowly sink onto his thickness. Once he's inside, I lean forward, slowly moving him in and out of me.

Aiden grabs my face and kisses me as I continue to move.

It feels good, but I'm not finding the friction I need to put me over the edge.

"Let me see you, Romy," Aiden says, gently pushing on my shoulders, so I lean back on my knees. "Do what makes you feel good, baby."

I start grinding against him as I move, which gives my clit precisely what it needs. Typically, in this position, I would feel self-conscious. I'd worry about if my boobs look saggy or if my stomach is jiggling too much, but right now, I don't feel the least bit judgmental about myself.

Instead, I feel sexy—like a fucking goddess. That's what Aiden does to me. He gives me the confidence that I never knew I could have. I feel more beautiful than I have ever have before—even back in my skinnier days.

My hands brace against his chest as I ride him. Now, I feel my orgasm starting to build. Every movement moves me closer to the release my body craves.

When Aiden's hands move to my breasts to play with my nipples, I lose all control. My steady, measured movements have turned into wild and crazy ones. I feel like I'm riding one of those mechanical bulls as I struggle to stay on while I'm coming.

I feel him tense and hear him let out a groan as he finishes too.

I collapse into a heap on top of him as he gently strokes my hair.

"Well, that was fun," I say breathlessly. "Time to go back to bed?"

Aiden kisses the top of my head. "Oh no, beautiful. I have big plans for us today."

# Chapter Twenty-seven

## AIDEN

When I arrived back to our room and I saw Romy in the shower, I just had to have her. I don't know what came over me.

Okay, yes, I do.

I'm a guy.

Once we are both up and dressed, Romy notices the plastic cups on the table.

She points over at them. "I think our coffee has gotten cold by now."

I laugh. "I'm sure it is. We can grab some more while we're out."

"And by 'out,' you mean?" She tries to pry more information out of me. I told her to get dressed for a day of fun but didn't give her any details.

Truth be told, although I have a couple of plans, I'm just sort of winging it. The only thing that I do know is that it's our last day, and I intend to make the most of it.

Romy bends over to pick up something on the floor, giving me a glimpse of her round ass. If she keeps doing that, we'll never get out of this room.

She's wearing some jean cut-off shorts with a light blue tank top with some sort of thin gold chain attached to it. She's got her hair down and in loose waves.

She looks beautiful—as usual.

But we have a day to get started. So, five minutes later, we are out the door. I take her hand in mine and hold it down the elevator and into the lobby.

Before we hit the front door, a man calling my name and jogging toward us gets my attention.

A middle-aged man with salt and pepper hair approaches us. Not wanting to be rude, we wait to see what he has to say.

"Aiden Montgomery," the man greets, holding out his hand. "Jason Rush. Nice to meet you."

I shake his hand. "Back at you, Mr. Rush. You need no introduction."

"So, you've heard of me?" He asks with a smile.

Oh yeah, I've heard of him. Rush Construction is one of the most prominent players in Minnesota.

Scratch that.

It *is* the most prominent player. And this man sits at the helm of it all. But from what I hear, he didn't start his empire with nothing but hard work. Word around town is that he had to sell his soul to a few devils to get where he is today.

Instead of saying any of that, though, I just respond with, "Of course. I think everyone in Minnesota has heard of you and your business."

He gives me the most shit-eating grin I've ever seen. "True, but from what I hear, you're quickly gaining on me."

*Damn straight.*

"Oh, I don't know about all that," I lie.

He pulls a business card out of his pocket and hands it to me. "How about when you get home, you give me a call? Maybe we can join forces on a project or two."

The man isn't great at subtlety.

I respond with, "I'll see what I can do. You know, if things slow down a bit. Been pretty busy."

He chuckles. "That's what I hear. Just think it over. I'm sure I can make it very *lucrative* for you."

I simply nod, and Romy and I head for the door once more.

When we are in our rental car, driving away from the resort, Romy asks, "Who was that guy?"

"Trouble," I answer.

We head into town, admiring the gorgeous views along the way. I knew Key West is a major tourist trap, yet somehow, it still has a small-town feel.

My hand rests on Romy's thigh the entire way, and there is a certain ease to it all.

I find a central place to park to walk around and aren't too far away from anything.

When we step out of the car, I ask, "Where do you want to start, beautiful?"

She turns her head back and forth, looking up and down the street. "You think we could find a souvenir shop? I want to grab something for Veronica."

I laugh. "Sweetheart, I think that's the bulk of these shops."

Grabbing her hand, I lead her to the shop that looks the biggest. Once inside, we walk around to pick out a shot glass for her friend and a mug for herself.

When we're about to leave, she stops. "Go on outside," she says. "I forgot something."

I'm about to tell her I'll go with her, but she's already hurrying off.

I take a seat on one of the benches, and people watch for a few minutes while I wait. I see a few other couples walk by. I see a father and son riding their bikes and a group of joggers all running in step. I wonder who lives here and who else is just on vacation.

It doesn't take long for Romy to reappear. I can't help but smile at the mere sight of her. She skips over to me with two bags in her hand. She grabs one of them and gives it to me.

"What's this?" I ask.

"Just a little something for you." She grins.

My fingers open the bag, and I reach inside, pulling out a navy blue baseball cap with **Key West** embroidered on the front.

She says, "I thought you could use a new one. The one you wear at work has gotten sort of gross. And I thought maybe when you wear it, you can think of this trip—and you know, think of me."

I use my thumb to trace the letters on the front of the hat. I don't know that I've ever had such a thoughtful gift.

When I don't answer for a moment, she gets nervous. "Oh no, you hate it."

Taking her by the hand, I pull her into my lap. Not caring who's watching, I lean in to kiss her.

When I pull back, I say, "No, baby, I love it. I'll wear it every damn day."

And I've never meant anything more.

# Chapter Twenty-eight

## ROMY

"These might be the best pastries I've ever had," I say with my mouth full.

Aiden and I are eating breakfast at a cute little cafe overlooking the water. We ordered a couple of coffees and a tray full of pastries. I'm pretty sure if I keep eating them, my ass is going to double in size.

I look across the table at Aiden, who is looking out over the ocean. He's wearing a plain white t-shirt and a pair of jeans, but he's still sexy as hell. He's got his hair pulled back into a low ponytail—the ends of it are blowing in the breeze. And to top it all off, he's wearing his new hat.

There's something about him wearing something I got him that makes me feel a little territorial. It makes me want to puff out my chest and chase off any other female that comes near him.

But I won't do that because, after today, he won't be mine anymore. I got him the hat almost as a goodbye—a nice reminder of our fleeting time together.

I just hope I don't get sad every time I look at it.

Trying to push away the bad thoughts, I decide to break the silence between us.

"So, who was the guy that stopped us earlier?" I ask.

"I'm sure you've heard of Jason Rush," he says.

Okay, guilty. I have heard of him, but I'm not sure what he wanted.

"And he wants to partner up with you on some projects?" I ask.

Finishing the bite in his mouth, he shakes his head back and forth. "He's not looking to partner up with me."

"Then, why did he—?"

He cuts me off. "He's trying to buy me out. As of late, I've been his biggest competition. He's trying to use us working together as an excuse to squash me like a bug. This isn't the first offer I've had to buy the company, so I'll go away."

I take a sip of my coffee. "Do you ever think about it?"

"Think about what?" His brow furrows.

"About selling. About sitting back and counting a huge stack of money."

"Nah, I've worked too damn hard to get where I am, and I wouldn't know what to do with myself if I wasn't going to work every day. Plus, I'd miss seeing my cute assistant." He winks and gives me a panty-melting smile.

I just hope he still feels that way after we end this whole thing.

**\*\*\*\*\*\*\*\*\*\*\*\*\*\*\*\*\*\*\*\*\*\*\*\*\*\*\*\*\*\*\*\*\*\*\*\*\***

After breakfast, we hit a couple more stores—more browsing rather than buying anything. We hold hands and talk and laugh. It's nice.

I'm going to miss it.

But I try not to think about that.

Instead, I try to enjoy our time together and try to pretend that tomorrow doesn't exist.

While walking around, we find a random hole-in-the-wall arcade and duck into play some games.

"Are you ready to lose?" Aiden asks as we walk over to a row of Ski Ball machines.

I look all around me, even bending down to peek under one of the machines.

"What are you doing?" He asks.

"Oh, sorry. I was just looking around for who you were talking to."

His laugh booms loud enough to make a few people turn around to look at us.

Each of us takes a spot in front of a machine and puts in our tokens. The machines spring to life, and the gate opens, sending the balls flying down the chute.

We both pick up one of the smooth brown balls. We pull our arms back and release them at the same time.

Mine flies into the top right corner, sinking into one of the 100k point pockets.

Aiden's clips the side of one of the smaller holes, but it flies out, and he gets zero points. He looks over at me, and I try not to smile.

Each of us picks up another ball. This time, I hit for 50k. And Aiden? He gets 5k.

The rest of the games goes on like that, and I win by a landslide. I tell myself not to gloat, but I can't help but do a little victory dance.

He turns toward me. "Okay, what's the deal? How did you get so good at Ski Ball? I think I just got hustled."

"When I was younger, my parents weren't around, so I would walk down to the local arcade and play. I was there every day after school, playing Ski Ball. I got so good that kids would bet me a dollar they could beat me. I'd face opponent after opponent, but I'd win every time. Kids from all around the neighborhood would come to watch." I use my hands to gesture as I talk.

Aiden's eyes are as big as saucers. "Whoa! Seriously?"

The dam breaks, and I can't contain it anymore. My lips curl into a smile, and I bust out laughing.

"No, Boss Man, none of that is true. I'm just freakishly good at Ski Ball."

Those wide eyes of his? They're now rolling at me. "Oh, you're so full of shit."

We both laugh, and he pulls me in for a hug and a kiss on

the cheek.

With a quick smack to my ass, he says, "Come on, beautiful. Let's go find something I can beat you at."

# Chapter Twenty-nine

## AIDEN

"Aiden, I'm sorry, but this just isn't going to work," I hear Romy say behind me. "Time to say goodbye."

*Damn.*

When I turn around, I'm faced with the barrel of her laser tag gun.

"Don't move," she warns.

Dramatically, I say, "So, this is how it ends—the end of an era."

"Any last words?" She asks.

In one swift motion, I knock her gun out of the way and push her against the wall behind her. My mouth attacks hers like it's on a mission.

Her body relaxes against mine as we make out under the glow of the black lights. I hope no kids are running by because if they are, they're getting quite the show.

Romy intensifies the kiss and uses one hand to fist the collar of my shirt. I feel her other hand lift, and I wait for it to wrap around my neck like it always does.

But the only thing I feel is the vest strapped to my chest start to vibrate.

Looking down, I see it light up, and my mouth falls open. "You shot me. I was kissing you, and you shot me."

She pokes her finger into my chest. "Don't play with me,

Boss Man. I know the only reason you were kissing me was to keep me from shooting you. Didn't work."

I can't help but laugh. "Are you always this competitive?"

Her brow furrows. "Yes. Always."

We head toward the door and return our vests and guns. Romy and I have had so much fun today. We've acted like a couple of kids—playing games at the arcade, searching for shells on the beach, and playing laser tag against each other.

Hanging out with Romy is more fun than I've had in a long time—maybe ever. She has a way of brightening my grumpy disposition like my little ray of sunshine.

After we leave laser tag, I glance at my phone to check the time.

Seeing it's later than I thought, I say, "Come on, we have to hurry, or we will miss the boat."

"Boat?" She asks. "Are you being metaphorical?"

We hurry over and get in the rental car to head toward our destination.

"So, are you going to tell me where we are going?" Romy pesters.

"Can't you be patient?

Her hands fly up in the air. "No! Haven't we established that by now?!"

I point at things out the window to try to distract her. It only half works, but thankfully, it's less than a ten-minute drive.

I park in a small lot across from a dock. When we get out of the car and head that way, she sees where we're going.

"We're going on a boat?" She beams.

"Do you like boats?"

"I don't know. Never been on one."

I stop walking. "You've never been on a boat?"

She shakes her head.

"Well, you're in for a fun night then," I promise before continuing to walk.

I just hope she doesn't get seasick.

We walk down the dock and step onto the boat. I show our

144

reservation confirmation to the captain and the attendant while Romy looks out over the edge.

The two men introduce themselves, and a few minutes later, we are out on the water.

There's a small table set up, covered up with a clean white tablecloth. We sit across the table from each other as the sun begins to set. It's beautiful, but looking at Romy, I think I have the better view.

The attendant, Charles, gives us two flutes filled with champagne. I hold mine up and ask, "What should we toast to?"

She wiggles her lips back and forth as she thinks before holding up her glass. "Let's toast to the end of a perfect week."

That sounds like a statement, signaling the beginning of the end.

But I clink my glass against hers all the same.

A few minutes later, Charles reappears with two massive plates—each containing a beef fillet, a lobster tail, and a baked potato.

Romy's eyes light up. "Wow, you went all out, Boss Man."

"Only the best for you," I reply, shooting her a wink.

She rolls her eyes but still smiles. Mission accomplished.

We eat and admire the view as the boat skims the waves.

Once we've finished, Charles takes all plates and disappears below deck. The captain is steering the boat, but he's out of earshot. I figure now is as good of a time as any to talk.

I begin with, "I know both of us have been avoiding this conversation, but I think we should talk."

"About what?"

"About what happens when we go back home—between you and me."

Her gaze falls to her lap. "I guess we go back to how things were before. This week has been wonderful, but we decided it was just for the week, right?"

The words cut me like a knife. I thought we were on the same page.

"Is that really what you want?" I ask.

She still avoids any eye contact as she nods.

I say, "Romy, it would be easier to believe that if you were looking at me while you said it."

Her eyes finally meet mine. "Aiden, we decided from the start that this thing had an expiration date on it. And as perfect as this week has been, I think we should stick to it."

When I don't immediately respond, she goes on. "Aiden, you and I have a great working relationship, and I don't think we should do anything to ruin that. I *really* need this job. I can't risk losing it."

The way she says she needs this job makes me think something is going on that she's not telling me, but I don't press her about it.

Because at the end of the day, she said she wants this thing to be over. And I made a promise that I wouldn't do anything to make her feel uncomfortable. I meant every word of it.

I could sit here and be a dick about it, or I could enjoy our last night together.

She squirms in her seat, and the look on her face looks like she's trying to decide whether she should jump ship or swim for shore.

"Hey," I begin. "You don't have to worry. I understand. After tonight, all goes back to normal."

Her eyes finally look back at me. "Are you sure?"

I nod. "Of course. At least we will always have Key West." I give her a reassuring smile.

Relief washes over her features. "Yes, we will always have Key West," she giggles.

"But Romy?"

"Yeah?"

"Tonight, you're *mine.*"

# Chapter Thirty

## ROMY

We are barely through the door before Aiden's mouth descends upon mine. The kiss is wild and frenzied—both of us fighting to make the most of it.

His hands seem to be everywhere all at once, and my head spins with all the sensations. His mouth leaves mine just long enough to pull my shirt over my head. Mere seconds later, he's got my bra unhooked and ripped from my body.

My breasts feel heavy as he toys with them. I squeal as he pinches my nipples between his fingers. It feels incredible, but if he doesn't stop with the teasing, I'm going to have a freaking lake in my panties.

His hands move from my breasts to my arms, pinning them above my head before his mouth takes over where his hands left off. His tongue circles my nipple, and I struggle to stand still.

My fingers twitch with the urge to touch him, but they're still secured above my head. When he finally lets them go, it's only so he can lead me to the bed. Once he lays me down, he wastes no time in getting rid of my shorts.

He positions himself so his face is inches from my pussy. I'm anxious to feel him inside me, but when he runs his finger up and down my slit, I know I'm in for more teasing.

"Please, Aiden," I whine. "Fuck me."

"Baby, this is our last night together. I'm not going to let it pass by without tasting this sweet pussy one last time."

Before I can say another word, he devours my pussy. He licks, laps, and sucks like it's his favorite thing in the entire world.

My legs tremble as the pressure inside me builds. Feeling bold, I look down at him, watching as he does those mind-blowing things with his mouth.

I now understand the appeal of men watching girls giving them head. It's sexy as hell.

When he sucks my clit like a damn vacuum and rolls his tongue back and forth over it, I lose my mind. My orgasm hits me like a freight train.

I grab his hair, holding him in place as I ride out my release on his face. I come for what feels like hours.

When I've stilled, he places one final soft kiss on my pussy, and I jump from the sensitivity.

Aiden stands up and undresses so quickly that when he slides inside me, I'm still feeling the aftershocks from my orgasm. The walls of my wet channel tighten around him as he starts to pump in and out.

My nails dig into his shoulders as I try to savor this moment.

I try to take a mental snapshot of everything about this moment.

The way Aiden feels inside me.

The way he looks at me.

How his kiss feels against my lips and on my skin.

All of it. I want to remember all of it. Every. Last. Detail.

It may have only been a week, but damn, I'm going to miss having Aiden this way. As we have sex, it feels like it's been so much longer than just a week.

I wish we could go home and try to make a go of things, but there's just too much at stake. It's too big of a risk.

Emotion threatens to overtake me as I feel tears stinging behind my eyes, but I do my best to force them back. I don't want him to see how much this is killing me.

Instead, I pull him close and kiss him, trying my hardest to get lost in the moment once again and not think about tomorrow. I try to forget about the fact that I'm head over heels in love with Aiden Montgomery.

Because it doesn't matter. All that matters right now is him and I.

Us.

# Chapter Thirty-one

## ROMY

I toss my suitcase down as I enter my apartment. I've always loved my quaint little home, but now, it seems much more empty and cold than when I left.

I tell myself that it's because I haven't had a moment alone in the past seven days. People have constantly surrounded me.

Yes, that's what I tell myself while ignoring the nagging in my voice, saying it's just *one* person in particular that I miss.

Even this morning, Aiden was wonderful to me. Before we boarded the plane, he stopped and kissed me one final time.

He said he had to savor one last kiss before we left paradise.

*Have I mentioned how perfect he is?*

He insisted on driving me home since his truck was parked at the airport. It was a quiet ride, but he didn't make it uncomfortable.

When he stopped in front of my apartment building, it took every ounce of my willpower to be able to step out of the vehicle and walk inside.

Before we went on this trip, I thought I was happy with my life. Now, it seems somewhat…lacking.

I let out a loud sigh even though there's no one around to hear it. Even in my thoughts, I sound ridiculous.

I just need a couple of days, and I'll feel normal.

Right?

I mean, I have to. There's no other option. I still have to work with this man.

I just need time. They say time heals all wounds—or some sort of bullshit like that.

Walking further into the apartment, I see a brown envelope sitting on my small kitchen table. The pit in my stomach starts to come back with full force.

I can't avoid its contents forever, but I will avoid them a bit longer while I take a shower.

*********************************************

I spend way longer than I should under the hot spray of the showerhead. I stay in there until the hot water turns frigid. I think I was hoping it would wash away the funk I'm in.

Didn't work.

So, I pour a glass of wine, hoping for a better result. Once I have my overly full glass, I take a seat on the couch, and my fingers pry open the top flap of the envelope.

I spend the next hour going through all the paperwork, trying to make sense of all the legal jargon.

If I understand it correctly, the gist is that my father is now being charged with crimes regarding all of the offshore accounts. But I don't know what any of this has to do with me—aside from the accounts being in my name.

Okay, that looks bad.

Along with the paperwork in the envelope, there's a business card.

**FBI AGENT TOM CARLSON**

Before the effects of my wine have worn off, I grab my phone and punch in the numbers that are printed on the small white card. I twirl it between my fingers as the phone rings.

On the third ring, I hear, "Agent Carlson."

"Uhm, hi," I stammer. "This is Romy Sinclair. You left some paperwork for me."

I probably should have thought about what I was going to say before I made the call.

But he doesn't seem to care. "Yes, Miss Sinclair! Thank you for reaching out."

Still unsure of what to say, I answer with, "Mm-hmm."

"I have some things I'd like to go over with you if you wouldn't mind coming in to talk to me."

"That depends. Are you going to arrest me?" And there's the wine talking.

He chuckles. "No, I don't think so. I just have some questions about your father. It shouldn't take too long. You let me know a time that works for you."

I tell him I'm off tomorrow, so we settle on a time, and he gives me directions.

I hang up the phone, and I can't tell if I'm relieved or even more nervous than before.

And the only person I want to talk to about all of it, I can't. Okay, that's not true. I'm sure I *could* talk to Aiden about every bit of this.

But I won't.

# Chapter Thirty-two

## AIDEN

This morning, I woke up feeling like shit—and not just from missing Romy—although that's part of it. I'm pretty sure I picked up a cold on the plane, turning my nose into an on-demand snot machine.

I've spent the better part of the morning lying on the couch, watching a marathon of a tv show where they build an insanely cool treehouse.

A commercial comes on for some sort of coconut hair oil, and immediately, I'm reminded of Romy. It seems like everything reminds me of her.

Part of me is excited to go back to work tomorrow to keep my mind on something else. Then again, Romy is there too, so maybe that won't work.

All the way home, she acted like she was torn—like she was reconsidering her decision about this whole thing. I was tempted to pull her close and kiss her until she changed her mind.

I doubt it would've taken much convincing, but I let her walk away.

I'm trying to be angry with her—to find a way to make this whole thing go away. I just can't bring myself to be mad at her, though.

Man, I'm in deep for this woman. And she is just going to

leave me twisting in the wind.

# Chapter Thirty-three

## ROMY

"Thank you for coming down, Miss Sinclair," Agent Carlson pulls out a chair for me to sit on.

"Please call me Romy," I say, trying to distance myself from my father's last name.

"Okay, Romy," he smiles and sits down across from me, opening a file that sits in front of him. "Can I get you anything? Coffee?"

"No, thank you. I'd just like to get on with this if you don't mind."

He nods. "Of course. As I'm sure you've seen from the paperwork, your father had some offshore accounts that have come to light. I'm interested in knowing your involvement with said accounts."

I sigh. "He told me about the accounts, but I've never touched them."

"Why did he put them in your name?"

"He told me the money was for me, but I think he's full of shit."

Agent Carlson's eyebrows shoot up. "Why's that?"

"Because he had those accounts before he was locked up. I do not doubt that if he hadn't gone to jail, he'd have kept that money all for himself."

He writes something down in that small notebook.

I continue, "Agent, can we cut the crap?"

He looks up from his notes. "Sure."

"My father is a bastard—always has and always will be. I don't want his money, and you've seen my apartment. Does it look I've touched any of that money?"

He cracks a slight smile.

Reaching into my bag, I pull out a stack of envelopes and slide them across the table. "This is every letter my father has written to me since he's been in prison. And there's a copy of the one letter I sent to him, telling him I don't want his money. I'm sure the prison will have a copy of that correspondence."

He takes the letters from me.

"Am I in some sort of trouble?" I ask. "What can I do to clear my name?"

"All of this should be sufficient. You're not our target. Your father and his organization are. Do you know anything about any of the other players he was working with?"

I laugh. "My father has barely spoken to me my entire life. I'm not even sure I know what his middle name is. I have no information besides what I've already given you."

"Fair enough."

"So, are we done?"

He nods. "Just one more question. Would you be willing to testify in court against your father?"

"Just tell me when and where."

\*\*\*\*\*\*\*\*\*\*\*\*\*\*\*\*\*\*\*\*\*\*\*\*\*\*\*\*\*\*\*\*\*\*\*\*\*\*\*\*\*\*\*\*\*\*\*\*\*\*\*\*\*\*\*\*\*\*

On my drive home, relief washes over me. I guess I won't be needing to hire that lawyer after all.

Leave it to me to make mountains out of molehills.

I feel like a huge weight has been lifted off my chest.

I should have known my father would still be making trouble for me. I don't know that he'll ever stop. I hope that he spends the rest of his life rotting in his 10x10 cell.

Pulling out my phone, I know I should make a phone call. It's not one I want to make, but I know I should.

Even though I know I'll probably hate myself, I press the

button and wait for it to ring.

It only takes two rings for the voice on the other end to answer with a chipper, "Hello?"

"Hi, Mom," I say, exhaling a deep breath.

"Who is this?"

I scoff. "Mom, it's Romy. Your *only* child. Who else calls you Mom?"

*I guess maybe her super young boyfriends might.*

*Gross.*

"I just didn't recognize you, dear—considering it's been years since I've heard from my daughter."

*Shots fired.*

"Glad to know your snarky wit is still on point, Mom."

"Where do you think you got yours from, dear? Now, are you okay? Did someone die?" She asks, still with the sass.

"No, no one died. Just calling to see if you heard about Dad."

She pauses a moment. "What about your father?"

I explain to her everything that has gone on and say, "I just wanted to give you a heads up in case they come asking you questions too."

She sighs. "That man is such a piece of shit. I can't believe he did this to us."

*Us?*

I fight the urge to tell her that I think she's just as much of a piece of shit. I've never known the actual level of her involvement in my father's schemes, but I refuse to believe she was blind to it all. She's too smart for that.

Plus, my father might have been the one who made the money, but my mother typically handled the finances. And by 'handled,' I mean 'spent.'

I tune back into her rambling about how being with my father was the worst mistake of her life. Good to know since I was a product of their time together.

My parents were always wrong for each other. I don't have one memory of them being loving or caring to one another. They always were at war with each other—even if they tried to hide it. I'm honestly surprised they even got along long enough to conceive me.

The truth is that my mom wanted a sugar daddy, and my dad wanted a trophy wife. They each got what they wanted, yet they were still miserable.

I listen to her for a couple more minutes before making an excuse to get off the phone. Then, I vow that I won't make the same mistake of calling her again for a while.

My mind begins to wonder what my life would have been like if my parents loved each other? Would we have taken family vacations? Would we get together every Christmas for our lovely traditions? Would I look forward to conversations with them?

I don't know, but it's pointless to look back and play out worthless fantasies. Rehashing the past does nothing for your future. The only thing I can do now is to make sure I don't make the same mistakes in my own life.

I want to find someone I'm crazy about. Someone who is my best friend along with my partner. Someone who I have a real connection with.

A tiny voice in my head is saying that I already found that person in Aiden.

A pain hits me in the chest at just the thought of Aiden. I've been so worried about this whole debacle with the FBI and my father that I haven't had room in my brain for Aiden too.

But now that most of that worry is gone, my hunky boss is right back at the forefront of my thoughts. I don't know why. I mean, we had a great week together. That was it. We both agreed that it would be no strings attached.

*Then, why did he look heartbroken when we talked about it? And why am I missing him so much now?*

Maybe because he's damn near perfect—a man any woman would be lucky to have. But a man I want to keep to myself.

I'm fighting a mental war with myself because I want nothing more than to run into Aiden's arms and let him carry me off into the sunset.

But there's still one problem. He's still my boss, and I'm still his assistant. And we have an excellent working relationship that I don't want to fuck up.

*But maybe it wouldn't get fucked up. Maybe it would only get better.*

My head hits my seat as I try to knock some clarity into my brain.

I can't tell if it's working or not, but I do decide on something.

Tomorrow, I'm going to walk into work with an open mind—an open mind that just might consider the possibility of trying to make it work with my boss.

# Chapter Thirty-four

## ROMY

The following day, I have every intention of making myself look super cute to make sure I get Aiden's attention, but when I sleep through my alarm, that becomes impossible. So, my glasses, messy bun, and semi-casual clothes will have to do.

Aiden said he didn't care what I wore, right?

I fidget my entire way to work but not from nerves. I'm excited to see him. We've been apart for a day and a half, and I act like I haven't seen him in months.

When I pull into the parking lot of the job site, I take a moment to compose myself before walking in. The butterflies in my stomach have officially taken flight.

When I walk inside the small trailer, Aiden is already sitting at his desk, staring at his computer screen.

"Good morning," I say with a smile.

His eyes glance up at me for the briefest of moments. "Hi," he replies quietly.

I get settled in at my desk and start trying to get myself organized. There's a frigid silence between us, and I don't like it.

"How was the rest of your weekend?" I ask, trying to start some dialogue.

This time, he doesn't even look at me. "Fine."

I stare at him, searching for any sign of what might be

bothering me.

He's so cold that maybe silence would be preferable over this awkward song and dance we are doing.

But I've come too far to stop now. "Man, I had a crazy weekend. Wait until you hear what happened—"

He cuts me off. "Yeah, maybe later. Did you see this email about the Stevens project?"

My mouth hangs open like a freaking cartoon character. "Uh, no. Not yet," I stammer.

"It says we lost the contract."

"What?" I ask, pulling it up on my screen. "What happened? I thought we were good as gold on that."

"Yeah, me too, but it got snaked right out from under me while we were gone." He slams his hand down on the table, sending papers flying everywhere. "Fuck!"

I jump at his volume.

"Let me make some calls," I offer. "I'm sure we can lowball it and get it back."

Before I can utter another word, he's storming out. The door to the trailer bangs a few times from the Winter air blowing in. As cool as the air is, though, it's nothing compared to how cold this room was ten seconds ago.

******************************

The rest of the day carries on about the same. I don't see much of Aiden since he's out working with the other guys.

And when I do see him, he's just as much of a dick as he was this morning.

A major wave of sadness hits me when I realize he's not wearing the hat I bought him in Key West.

*So much for never taking it off.*

I try to do my job and not let him see how much this is affecting me.

Before our trip, Aiden was always a little grumpy, but he was never an outright jerk to me. He's always treated me as more of an equal rather than his assistant. Today is the first time I've really felt the definition of my title.

The only time he's spoken to me is when he needs me to do something work-related, and although I know that's my job, it doesn't make this any less difficult..

He promised me nothing would change. He promised me everything would be okay—no matter our relationship status.

I guess we aren't fucking anymore, so he doesn't have to be nice. I feel so stupid.

*This* is why sleeping with your boss is a bad idea. How could I have done something so reckless?

And what if it never gets any better? I don't know that I can deal with this version of Aiden forever.

Standing up, I walk over to make myself a cup of coffee. My eyes are drawn to the small window not far from where I'm standing.

Aiden is walking by with Tom, his second in command.

The windows in the trailer are thin enough that I can eavesdrop.

I hear Tom say, "So, the Stevens job fell through?"

Aiden nods.

"What the hell happened?"

Aiden sighs. "Fucking Jason Rush. He saw me at the conference and had his people sneak in with a lower bid."

"We can't play ball with them? Make them a better deal?"

This time, he shakes his head. "No, if I bid any lower, we'd lose money. I've got a bottom line to meet."

I've looked at the financials, so I know what he's saying is true.

"I'm sorry, man. That job would have been huge for us. Guess you shouldn't have gone on that trip, huh?" He gives a joking laugh.

I wait for Aiden to say something to defend our time together, but it never comes.

Instead, he says, "Yeah, no joke. Live and learn."

Tears burn behind my eyes because that trip meant everything to me, and clearly, it meant nothing to him.

Or maybe it meant something to him too, but he turned

bitter when I didn't want to keep it going.

Out the window, I can see Aiden coming back inside, so I hurry back to my desk as though I wasn't just being nosey.

I try my hardest to hold back tears as he comes in and grabs his keys off the desk. "I'm leaving for the day," he growls before flying back out the door.

The second it shuts behind him, my tears begin to fall freely. This place, this job that used to be home, now feels like my hell.

Aiden was right about one thing: that trip was a huge fucking mistake.

# Chapter Thirty-five

## AIDEN

I'm almost all the way home before guilt eats at me enough that I turn back around.

Ever since I woke up, today has been the day from hell. Everything that *could* have gone wrong *did* go wrong. I woke up late and then spilled coffee on the hat Romy got me. Then, I got a flat tire on my way to work and found out we lost the Stevens job once I got there.

And to top it all off, I still feel like shit and can't seem to shake this cold.

But none of that is an excuse for how I treated Romy. I took my bad day out on her, and it wasn't right.

Earlier, she even tried to tell me something eventful about her weekend, and I completely blew her off.

The truth is, I was a total dick for no good reason. She probably thinks I hate her for her decision about our relationship—or lack thereof.

But that has nothing to do with it. I meant it when I told her that nothing would change, but then she comes in, and I'm sure it seemed like everything had changed.

Honestly, I'm not mad at her. Although my feelings were hurt, anger never played a part in it. And when I came home from Key West and cleared my mind, I was able to see that something was bothering her. I'm not sure if it was me or something else entirely—and I didn't ask like I should have.

Maybe if I had, I could've helped her through it—or at least listened. And maybe things would have turned out differently.

*Maybe.*

Either way, I'm on my way back to the office to apologize, and I hope to catch her before she heads home for the night.

I spend the rest of the drive trying to think of what I'm going to say to her and about what an idiot I've been. My head is still fuzzy from the cold medicine I took around lunchtime, so it makes it hard to focus on anything too long, but I try.

When I get to the job site, some of the guys are finishing up for the day, and they all wave and say hello as I park and make my way into the trailer.

I bust through the door, hoping to see Romy sitting at her desk, but she's not there.

*Damn.*

I should've looked for her car in the parking lot before I came in, and I could've saved myself some disappointment.

I walk over to her desk and notice something. It's not just that Romy is gone, but she took all of her stuff with her. The only things that are left are her monitor, docking station for her laptop, and a folded piece of paper.

The outside of the paper is labeled: **Mr. Montgomery**

My fingers practically rip the paper as I open it to read. My eyes struggle to focus.

**Mr. Montgomery,**

**I realize this is probably the most unprofessional way I could possibly do this, but I'm giving you my resignation.**

**I thought that we could come back from our trip, and everything would go back to normal. I felt that even if we left the romantic stuff on that beach, maybe we could bring the bond we formed back with us. Hell, I was even entertaining the idea of...more.**

**But now, I see that you can't put the genie back in the bottle. God, I wish we could because I'll miss this job so very much.**

I'm sorry for not giving more notice and for leaving you hanging, but I don't think the uncomfortable situation between us is very good for your business.

I've emailed you a list of phone numbers and passwords —everything you'll need to handle things without me. I hope you find a great assistant to replace me—someone who has a tougher skin. And someone who won't throw herself at you when she's drunk.

I wish I could do this, but I just can't. And I know it's all my fault. I'm sorry to leave you in a bind. I'm sorry I didn't know what I wanted when it mattered most.

But most of all, I'm sorry I kissed you on that beach.

-Romy

# Chapter Thirty-six

## ROMY

"**G**o away!" I groan from my couch.

The pounding on my door continues, and Veronica shouts, "You have exactly ten seconds to open this door, or I'm going to call the super and tell him I smell a gas leak, so he'll let me in."

When I don't get up, she starts counting, "Ten! Nine!"

Sighing and rolling my eyes, I get up to unlock the door. Veronica has a key, but I had the deadbolt and the chain locked.

"What?" I say, swinging the door open.

"Don't 'what' me, Romy Sinclair! You quit your job after your vacation with your boss and won't give me any details. Romy, you love that job. What the hell happened on that trip?"

I leave the door open and walk back to the couch.

"Everything," I mumble.

She shuts the door behind her and follows me to the couch. I've already flopped down, taking up the length of it, so she lifts my feet, setting them in her lap as she sits.

"Talk to me, sweets," she says. "Tell me what happened."

Without warning, a tear streaks down my cheek. I cried that day I left Aiden the note, but I've just felt numb since then. All I do is order takeout, watch TV, and sleep.

But right now, all my emotion comes bubbling to the surface.

"I kissed him," I begin.

She doesn't utter a word but waits for me to continue.

"We were drunk, and I kissed him, which led to other stuff — *all* the other stuff. We had this agreement that we would spend the week with no strings attached, and it was perfect. It was like I'd been waiting all my life for a man like him."

Now, she speaks. "Let me guess; at the end of the week, he was ready to call it quits, and you weren't?"

I shake my head. "Just the opposite. I think he was ready to have a go at a real relationship, but I was the one who said no."

"You're going to have to give me more here, Romy, because it sounds like you had a great thing going."

"I got that news about my dad, and I started freaking out —worrying I shouldn't do anything to jeopardize my job since I'd probably have to pay for a lawyer."

She nods because I did text her to tell her about the outcome of my meeting with the FBI. "So, you jumped the gun?"

I rub my eyes. "Pretty much. So, then, I thought I'd go to work and talk to him—maybe tell him what had happened and why I did what I did. But he was so cold and distant. It was like he hated me or something. I just couldn't stay there, V."

"I get it, and I don't blame you. I've just never seen you like this. Romy, you didn't even act like this when that shit went down with your parents when we were in college."

*Maybe because Aiden means more to me than my shitty parents.*

When I don't say anything, she asks, "Have you tried talking to him since? Maybe it was all just a misunderstanding."

"No, V. I think I understood just fine, and I don't want to be put through that again."

The tone in my voice tells her not to push the issue.

She instead decides to change the subject. "Okay, Romy. Time for some tough love. You look like shit, and you smell even worse. You need to get up and go take a shower."

"Later," I mutter.

"No, now."

All I give in response is a loud scoff.

"Romy, we can do this one of two ways. You can go take a shower on your own, or I can bring a bucket of water and soap out here to dump on you."

"You wouldn't," I taunt.

"We both know I would."

She is right. She definitely would.

When I don't immediately respond, she says, "Plus, I have a surprise for you."

"Surprise?" My interest is piqued.

"Yep, a surprise. I'm going to go to my place and grab it, but so help me if you aren't clean by the time I get back, you won't get it."

"Okay, okay," I groan. "You win. I'll shower."

"The entire building thanks you," she replies with a healthy dose of sarcasm before she gets up and heads out the door.

\*\*\*\*\*\*\*\*\*\*\*\*\*\*\*\*\*\*\*\*\*\*\*\*\*\*\*\*\*\*\*\*\*\*\*\*\*\*

Half an hour later, I'm showered and back on my couch. I mindlessly flip through the channels, trying not to think about Aiden. I seem to be unable to escape him, though—especially when I see things like Star Wars on TV.

The past few days have been some of the worst of my life. Not only do I not have Aiden, but I don't have a job to go to— which makes me feel like I have no purpose.

I'm not just handling this whole 'life' thing very well at the moment.

Thankfully, I'm not trapped in my thoughts for long be- cause Veronica strolls back in. I don't immediately look at her, but I know it's her because she's talking from the moment she hits the door.

"Okay, Romy, I know you're probably going to kill me, but I know how depressed you've been, and I thought maybe you could use some company—someone to cheer you up."

*Oh lord, she brought me a guy. I'm so pathetic that she had to get me a man. That explains why she wanted me to shower!*

But when I sit up and turn around, she's not with a man. No, my best friend is standing all by herself—holding a small white ball of fluff in her hands.

The furry thing pokes its head up, and I see it's a dog. Maybe a long-haired terrier of some sort? I don't know. I'm not a dog guru.

But he's cute.

"It's a dog," I remark.

"Good job, Romy. You know what it is." Her snarky sarcasm comes through. "But it's not just any dog—it's *your* dog."

My eyes go wide. "You got me a dog?"

She nods.

"Why?"

"This lady I work with found him and has been taking care of him for a while, but she's got some health issues that have just come to light, so she can't keep him. He needs a good home."

"V, that answers why the dog needs a home. That doesn't explain why you brought it to me."

She sighs. "Because you both are going through a rough time, and you can help each other. And I'm tired of you sitting around, feeling like you have no purpose. And the number one reason? His name is Romeo. How kismet is that?! Romy and Romeo!"

Without warning, she hands him to me. I have to admit that he's pretty damn adorable. He has long hair which is a tan color, but the fur around his mouth is slightly darker, making him look like he's got a cute little mustache."

"V, he's super cute," I begin. "But I just quit my job, and I don't know that I can afford a dog."

"I knew you'd say that," she replies, walking back out into the hall. When she returns, she's holding a crate in one hand and a few bags in the other. "Which is why I've officially got you everything you need to get started. He's got a crate, two bowls, and enough food to last him a month. There are also treats and toys, and he's already been to the vet. Mr. Romeo has a clean bill of health and is up to date on all of his shots."

*Geez, she really did think of everything.*

She sets the stuff down and walks over to me. "Romy, I'm not taking no for an answer. You need something to be happy about."

I know all of this is coming from a good place, so I give a simple nod in response.

A wide smile spreads across her lips before she pulls me in for a hug. She then turns and heads for the door.

"Hey, where are you going?" I ask.

"I have to catch up on some stuff. I spent my whole day shopping for the dog." With another smile and a small wave, she's gone again.

I look down at Romeo, who looks like he can barely keep his eyes open.

"Don't worry, boy," I say. "I feel like that too when she leaves. Come on, let's introduce you to some trashy television."

# Chapter Thirty-seven

## AIDEN

"I hate paperwork," I growl to nobody but myself in the empty trailer.

The past week without Romy has been unbearable. I wish I could say it was just the paperwork that was the problem, but it's not. I miss everything about her, but instead of crying out my emotions, I've been a grumpy fuck all week—even more so than usual.

I've been putting in 14 hour days doing her job as well as my own, but I'm not even entertaining the idea of hiring a new assistant. That's a step I'm just not ready to take.

I continue to go through papers and send a few emails. An hour later, the door opens, and Tom pokes his head in.

"Hey Boss, there's someone here to see you."

My stomach does a flip at the thought that it might be Romy, but when I look up, a woman I don't recognize enters.

She's tall and lean with bright red hair and a scarlet dress to match. I bet the revealing outfit was enough to turn a few heads as she walked in here.

Tom sure as hell is staring at her like he wants a taste. I clear my throat to get his attention. When he sees me glaring at him, he steps out, closing the door behind him.

"Aiden, I assume?" The woman asks.

We take our seats on opposite sides of the desk.

Leaning back in my chair, I say, "I'm sorry, but you seem to know me, and I have no idea who you are."

She mimics me, leaning back in her chair. I bet those long legs of hers make most men drool—most men who aren't hung up on someone else.

"My name is Veronica."

My brain searches for who she is, and suddenly, it clicks. "Romy's friend?"

She nods.

"Is she okay?" I ask a little louder than I mean to.

"Depends on how you define 'okay'" she mumbles.

Before I can ask what she means, she continues, "Look, Aiden, I'm here because my best friend is miserable."

My eyebrows raise. "And that's my fault?"

"Yes."

I sigh. "Well, Veronica, I don't know if she told you this, but I'm the one who wanted more. She didn't because she didn't want to ruin our work relationship. And then, she quit her job."

I leave out the part about how I was a jerk when we came back to work.

"Oh, I'm aware of all of that," she replies. "She's being an idiot, but so are you."

I cross my arms over my chest, anxious to hear what she's going to say next.

"Romy wanted to keep things platonic because of some shit that happened while you guys were gone. She didn't want to do anything to mess up her job."

Now, I sit up in my chair. "What happened? Is she alright?"

She gives a wave of her hand as if pushing away the question. "She's fine. Everything worked out. She was coming around to the idea of starting something up with you—something real. Then, you went and acted like Mr. Dickhead."

"Oh, she told you about that?" I ask, feeling slightly embarrassed.

Veronica rolls her eyes. "Of course, she told me. Why do you think I'm here?"

"At this point, I'm not really sure why you're here. Why don't you enlighten me by getting to the point?" I ask.

"Aiden, I have seen my best friend at the worst points in her entire life—the lowest of the low." She pauses for a moment. "But never have I seen her as low as she is right now. She misses you, but she is way too damn stubborn to say it because she's scared of rejection, so I'm here to say it for her."

"So, she sent you?"

She laughs. "Hell no! She'd kill me if she knew I was here, but I had to come anyway. I'm just here to tell you that you both need to stop being stupid and get together already."

When I don't say anything—because I'm not sure what to say, Veronica gets up and heads for the door.

She turns toward me one last time. "Look, I didn't come here to bust your balls. I came here because I thought you might be missing her just as much as she misses you. If not, forget I was here. But I think you and I both know that a girl like Romy Sinclair doesn't come along very often."

With that, she's out the door, and I'm stuck trying to pick up my jaw off the floor.

Why wouldn't Romy tell me that something was going on while we were away? I would have been right there to help her fix it.

But that's not Romy, is it? She wants to handle everything herself. But I should have at least seen something was bothering her. Maybe if I had pressed harder, she would have told me.

I'd be lying if I said it didn't feel good that she was missing me like I'm missing her. The only thing that will make me feel really good, though, is having her back in my arms.

Without wasting another moment, I grab my jacket and head out the door, ready to make that happen.

# *Chapter Thirty-eight*

## ROMY

"**R**omeo, stop that," I command as he tries to eat his little hairbrush I'm attempting to use on him.

Instead, he runs around my bed in fast circles like a tiny torpedo. "What are you doing?" I laugh as he eventually slows down and lays right next to me with his belly up in the air.

I never thought I'd be a good dog mom, but here we are. Little Romeo has stolen my heart. And although he hasn't done much to make me stop missing Aiden, he at least makes my free time a little more enjoyable.

Plus, it's sort of nice having someone around to talk to who doesn't ever talk back. He's like a little therapist without all of the advice that we know I'm not going to take.

He even lets me snuggle him at night. Maybe I'll just keep the dog and forget about ever finding a man.

I've been actively looking for a job and am waiting for some perspectives to call me back. So, Romeo and I have spent our days playing, taking walks, and watching TV.

There's a knock on my door, and Romeo flips back over to look at me like, "What do we do?"

I know it's not Veronica because she's out of town. I figure it might be my super or something, so I stick Romeo in his crate for the time being—since I haven't exactly told my super that I have a dog.

"Okay, you have to be quiet, boy," I say, tossing a blanket over his crate.

Walking to the front door, I adjust my glasses, pushing them back up my nose. When I reach the door and swing it open, I think I just might faint.

Aiden Montgomery is standing in my doorway. He looks delicious in his dark jeans and black t-shirt, and holy hell, he's wearing the hat I got him!

I try to play it cool and not show any emotion, but I can't help but smile back when he smiles at me.

*Damn it, Romy!*

"Can we talk?" He asks.

I turn around to walk back into my living room, leaving the door open for him to follow me. It doesn't take him long.

I sit on the couch, but instead of taking a seat, he leans up against the wall opposite me. He just looks at me for a moment without saying a word, and I feel almost on display. I don't like it.

"Aiden, why are you here?" I ask.

I look away from his intense stare, but his next words bring my gaze right back to his.

"I'm in love with you, Romy. I think I've been in love with you for a long time, and I'm sorry it took me so long to realize it. I'm sorry it took us going away for a week for me to open my stupid eyes. And I'm sorry that when we came back, I didn't fight like hell to keep you."

Deep down, I know that no matter how hard he would have fought, I would have protested—because I'm an idiot.

"Aiden," I begin. "You weren't the one who walked away. You wanted this, and I left. And then at work, everything just felt messed up." I feel tears starting to prick my eyes as I realize I'm not making a ton of sense.

Walking over to me, he kneels in front of me, taking my hands in his. "Romy, there is no excuse for how I treated you that first day. I was just having a shitty day, and I took it out on you. I shouldn't have done it, and I'm sorry."

"Aiden, what are you saying?" I ask, my brain now in a full-on fog.

"I'm saying that I want to be with you. I want to wake up with you next to me every morning, and I want to go off to work with you. I want you in every aspect of my life. I'm saying I want you to be mine."

His words make me want to throw down every wall that I have and say screw everything else, but I know it's not that simple.

"Aiden, I don't know if we can just go back to how things were in Key West—I don't know if we can go back to the whole boss and assistant thing like they were before we left."

He shakes his head at me. "Romy, I'm not asking you to be my assistant. I'm asking you to be a partner in this business with me. I want to give you some equity because you've helped me grow it so much. You haven't been just my assistant for quite a while, and I think it's about time that I start showing that. And I need you to know that this offer to come back to work is not contingent on us being together. The job, the equity, all of it is yours if you come back to work—regardless of our relationship status. I just think it'd be nice to head off to work with you every day."

Now, I'm full-on crying. Thankfully, it's just quiet tears rather than the uncontrolled sobs I've been doing the past few days.

I try thinking of why this is a bad idea, and although there are a lot of them, the voice inside my head keeps saying that Aiden is worth the risk. For the past week, I've been wondering how great things could be if they turned out differently. And right here in front of me is the chance for them to truly be different.

I'm not about to pass that up.

Looking back at him, I say, "Well, it would be nice to be able to carpool in the mornings."

He grins. "So, you're saying—?"

"Oh, just kiss me, Boss Man."

Without wasting another second, he pulls me toward

him, crashing our lips together for what might be the best kiss I've ever had. We cling to each other for dear life as we barely want to stop long enough to breathe.

Feeling his kiss again makes me realize just how much I've missed it, and dear lord, I hope never to have to live without it again.

When we finally break apart, I take a second just to try to remember this moment. It still feels a little surreal.

He moves from the floor to the spot next to me on the couch. Before we go any further, I figure maybe we could talk a little more.

Deciding to give him a little shit, I say, "Aiden, there's something I need to tell you."

"Shoot, baby."

"While you and I were apart, I was…lonely. And I found someone to keep me company while I was alone."

His face drops a little, but he doesn't say anything. I stand up off the couch and walk into the bedroom. When I come back, I set Romeo down between us.

"This is Romeo," I say. "He might just take your place as the boss around here."

His laugh echoes off my apartment walls. "You got a dog?"

"Veronica got him for me."

He nods. "I need to confess something too, Romy."

Now, it's my face that drops.

"Veronica came to see me."

"What?"

"She came to see me to tell me how stupid she thought that we were both being. Romy, I wanted to come see you before now, but I didn't think that's what you wanted, so I stayed away. Veronica is the one who convinced me to give it one more time." He says it like he's worried any of that will change my mind.

"Aiden, I don't care what brought you here—as long as you're here now."

That sexy smile is back on his face, and he kisses me again. This time, he wastes no time in pulling me into his arms and carrying me into the bedroom.

Once we are in there, we practically rip each other's clothes off. As much as I want to take our time and savor this, there's no denying that both of us *need* this right now.

Before I know it, he's sliding into me. My moans fill the air between us as we fuck like animals. He angles my legs on his shoulders as he moves in and out of my pussy, and it's not long before I feel myself start to tighten around him.

When Aiden abruptly stops, I look up at him, wondering if he finished a little sooner than expected. But I don't think that's the case.

"What's wrong?" I ask.

He looks down at me, fighting back a smile. "Your dog just bit my ass."

I start laughing so hard that tears are streaming down my cheeks. "Are you okay?" I ask.

"I'm fine, but I think he thinks I'm hurting you," he laughs with me.

I hold up my finger, gesturing for him to wait a minute. Rolling out from under him, I grab Romeo and walk him over to his crate.

As I stick him in, I say, "Sorry, pup. Right now, he's the Boss Man."

# Chapter Thirty-nine

## AIDEN

*Six months later...*

"What the hell are you doing?" I ask Romy. I just walked into the construction trailer and saw Romy on her hands and knees under her desk. Her ass is sticking straight up in the air.

"Something under here came unplugged, and I'm trying to figure out what."

"Baby," I clear my throat. "I'm going to need you to come out of there."

"Why?"

"Because if you stay in that position, I'm going to take full advantage of it and pull your pants down and fuck you senseless."

The past six months have been amazing. After I came to her apartment that day, we've been inseparable. When we were spending every single night together, I convinced her that we should move in together, so we went and picked out a house—*our* house.

I made good on my promise to give Romy some equity in the company. Now we are official partners. I offered to buy some office space and let her work out of there, but she refused. In her words, "There's no way in hell I'm going to go to work every day without being able to stare at my hot boss."

She still calls me her boss even though it's not the case. The only place I want to be Romy's boss is the bedroom, and even then, she takes charge enough to tell me exactly what it is she wants.

So, since she didn't want an office space, I got her a top-of-the-line heater for the small trailers we work out of when it gets cold.

We've discussed marriage but have decided to wait until we take another vacation. Getting married on a beach in Key West seems like the perfect idea.

Little Romeo finally came around, and now, he's practically like our child. After talking about it, we eventually want kids of our own—the human kind—but neither of us is in any hurry. We are too busy enjoying our time together—and hopping into bed any chance we get.

Speaking of which, still on her knees, Romy wiggles her ass around.

"Oh no," she says. "I think I'm stuck. Maybe someone should come down here and teach me a lesson."

My dick instantly rises to the occasion. The woman still drives me just as insane as she did while we were away. Now, maybe even more so because I know she's all mine.

There's no expiration date on us now.

And I'll make sure there isn't one ever again.

"Romy," I warn. "Do you really want me to fuck you right here when anyone could just walk in and see it?"

She scoffs. "You and I both know that everyone is gone for the day, but I mean, if you don't want me, you don't *have to*—"

Now, she's baiting me.

And it works.

I kneel on the floor behind her, tugging her leggings down enough to expose her perfect ass.

"Really, baby?" I ask. "No panties again?"

Ever since our trip, she might as well have thrown all of her underwear away. She never wears them anymore. I'm not complaining, mind you—it still drives me just as wild.

I give her a quick swat to her ass before reaching between her legs to tease her clit. She moans and pushes against my hand. I rub her exactly the way she likes it.

As much as I want to fuck her right here and now, my knees are already starting to hurt. I must be getting old.

Instead, I decide just to make her feel good before taking her home to our king-size bed and having my filthy way with her.

The noises she's making let me know that she's close. I increase my tempo with one hand and use the other to grab ahold of her ponytail and hold her in place.

"Are you going to come for me, baby?" I ask, and it's as though a switch flicks inside of her, and her whole body quakes.

She's a little louder than I would like—at least in a spot where people might hear her. I rub her until her orgasm subsides before giving another swat to her ass.

"Come on, beautiful," I say. "Let's go home, and we can finish this there."

We both stand up, and she smiles up at me. Grabbing ahold of my shirt collar, she pulls me in for a kiss.

When she pulls back, there's a wicked look in her eyes. Putting on her jacket, she grins and says, "Whatever you say, Boss Man."

The end.

# Want to read about some sexy cowboys with filthy mouths?

Fall in love with the swoony, small-town guys of Grady.

Get Book 1 Here!
https://books2read.com/all-the-right-things

# Acknowledgement

Holy cow! This is book 10 for me! That seems so insane
to think about. I couldn't have done it without
some awesome people in my corner.

Thanks to Hannah...my ride or die...and my editor who isn't scared to tell me when something isn't working.

Thanks to Erica...the best PA a girl could ask for. She never ceases to amaze me with her dedication to all of us.

Thanks to the Peen Posse...You ladies are the best form of therapy.

Thanks to my husband...who supports me endlessly. I couldn't ask for a better partner in life.

Thanks to my ARC readers...you guys are amazing and always help mefind all the stupid little errors that slip though. I love you all so much.

And most of all, thank you to the READERS. You guys are making my dreams come true, and I'm forever grateful.

# Books by Stephanie Renee

Grady Romances
All the Right Things
All the Right Reasons
All the Right Choices
All the Right Moves (coming Fall 2021)

The Constant Series:
A Constant Surprise
A Constant Reminder
A Constant Love
A Constant Christmas (A holiday novella)

Spin-off Standalones
Seeing Red
Aces Wild

Anthologies
Cheaters (Coming April 2022)

Made in the USA
Columbia, SC
11 March 2024

32830123R00114